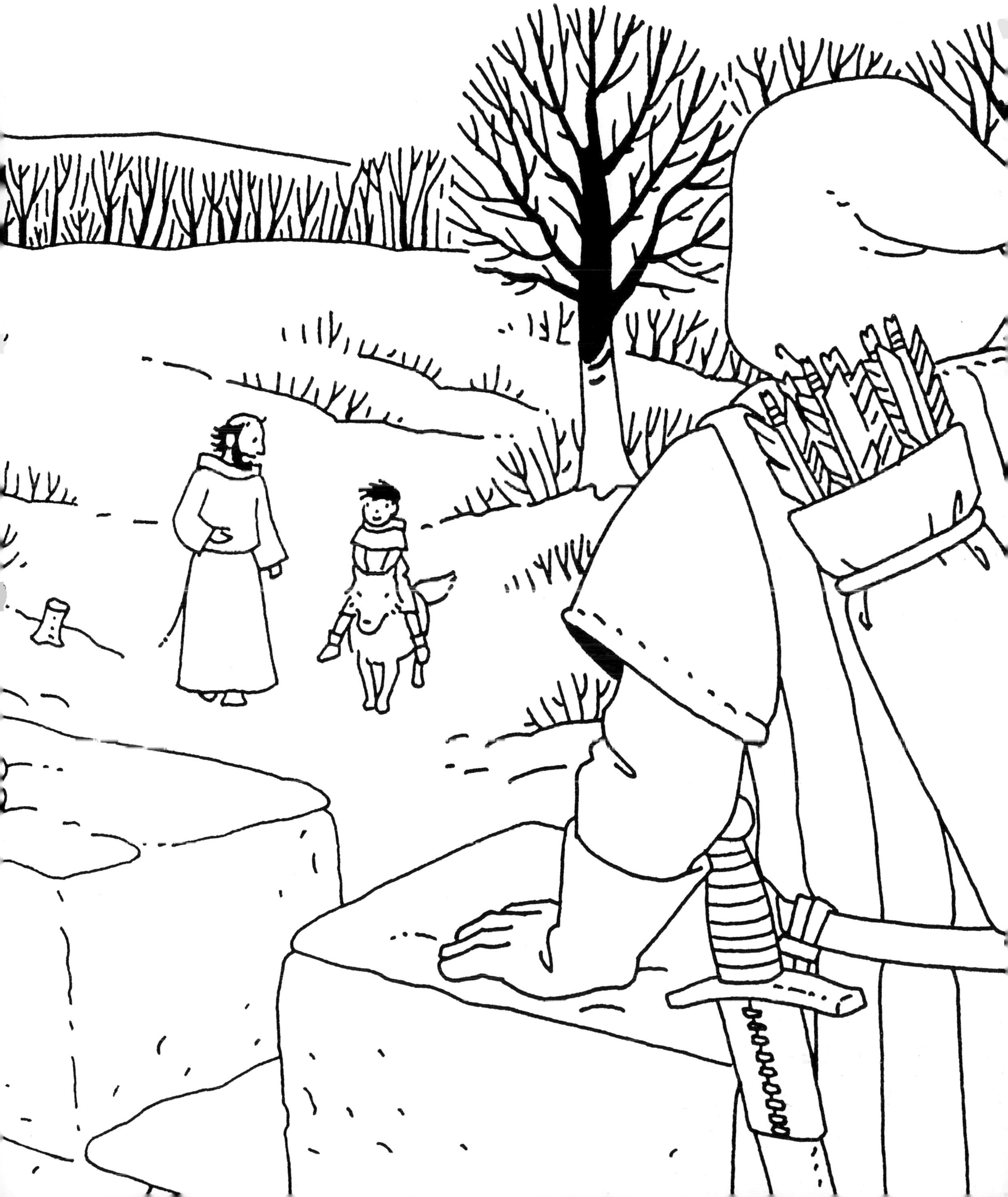

Jean-François Kieffer

The Adventures of LOUPIO

Translated by Carrie Akoun

VOLUME 1

The Encounter
and other stories

Ignatius

MAGNIFICAT.

Original French edition: *Les Aventures de Loupio*
Tome 1: La Rencontre et autres récits
© 2009 by Fleurus Mame, Paris
© 2010 by Ignatius Press, San Francisco • Magnificat USA LLC, New York
All rights reserved
ISBN Ignatius Press 978-1-58617-526-9
ISBN Magnificat 978-1-936260-12-6

The trademark MAGNIFICAT depicted in this publication is used under license
from and is the exclusive property of Magnificat Central Service Team, Inc.,
A Ministry to Catholic Women, and may not be used without its written consent.

Printed by Tien Wah Press,Singapore
Printed on July 19, 2010
Job Number MGN 10009

Table of Contents

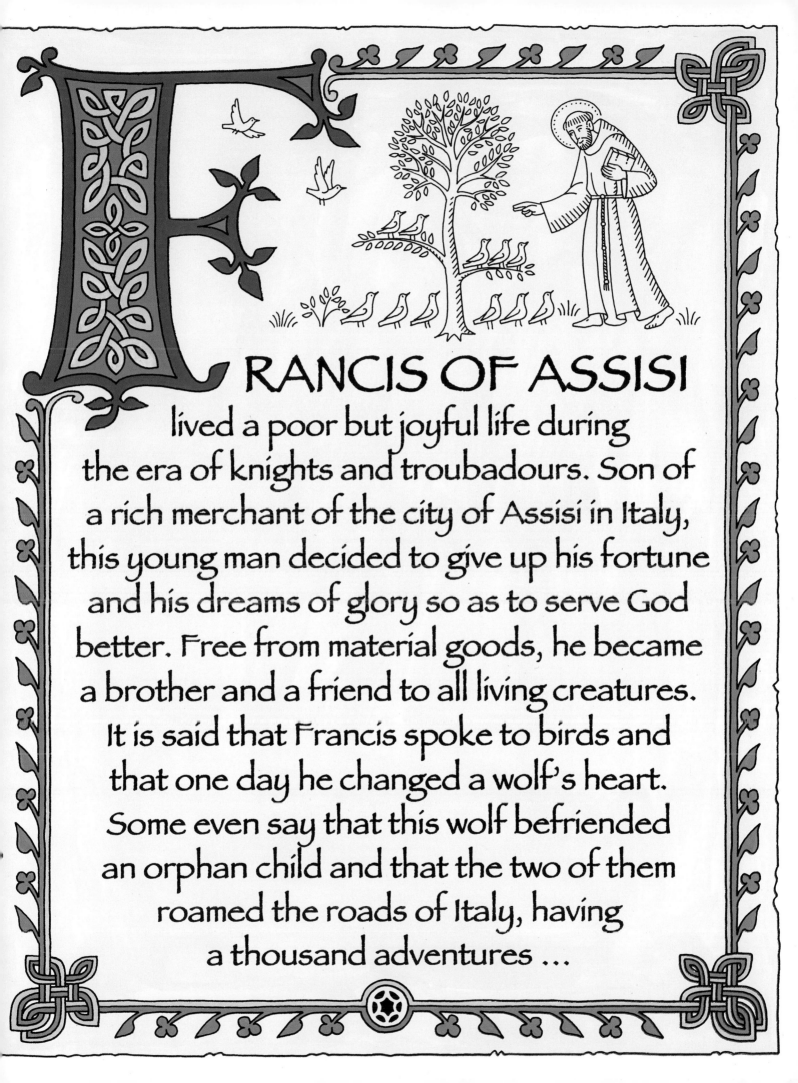

FRANCIS OF ASSISI

lived a poor but joyful life during
the era of knights and troubadours. Son of
a rich merchant of the city of Assisi in Italy,
this young man decided to give up his fortune
and his dreams of glory so as to serve God
better. Free from material goods, he became
a brother and a friend to all living creatures.
It is said that Francis spoke to birds and
that one day he changed a wolf's heart.
Some even say that this wolf befriended
an orphan child and that the two of them
roamed the roads of Italy, having
a thousand adventures ...

The Encounter

"IN THE DAYS WHEN SAINT FRANCIS LIVED IN THE TOWN OF GUBBIO, A LARGE AND TERRIBLE WOLF APPEARED IN THE LAND. IT WAS SO FEROCIOUS THAT IT DEVOURED NOT ONLY ANIMALS, BUT PEOPLE, TOO. NO ONE DARED VENTURE OUTSIDE OF THE TOWN ..."

The Little Flowers of Saint Francis, chap. 21

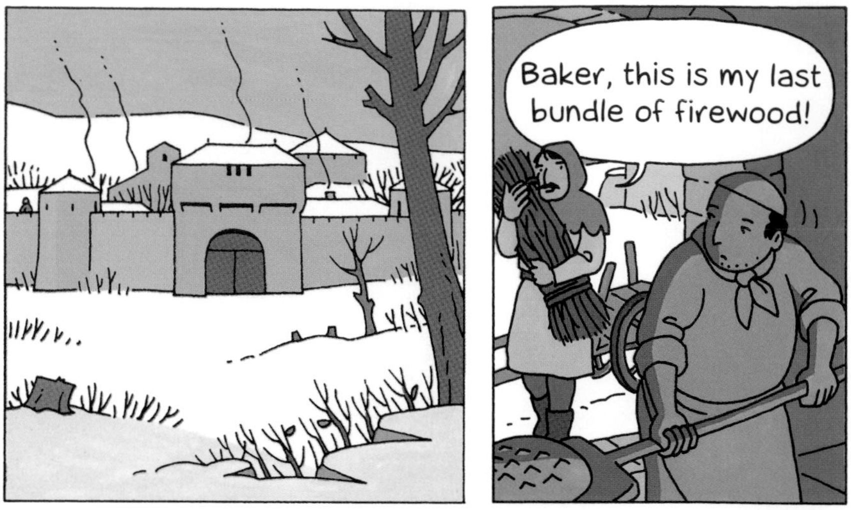
Baker, this is my last bundle of firewood!

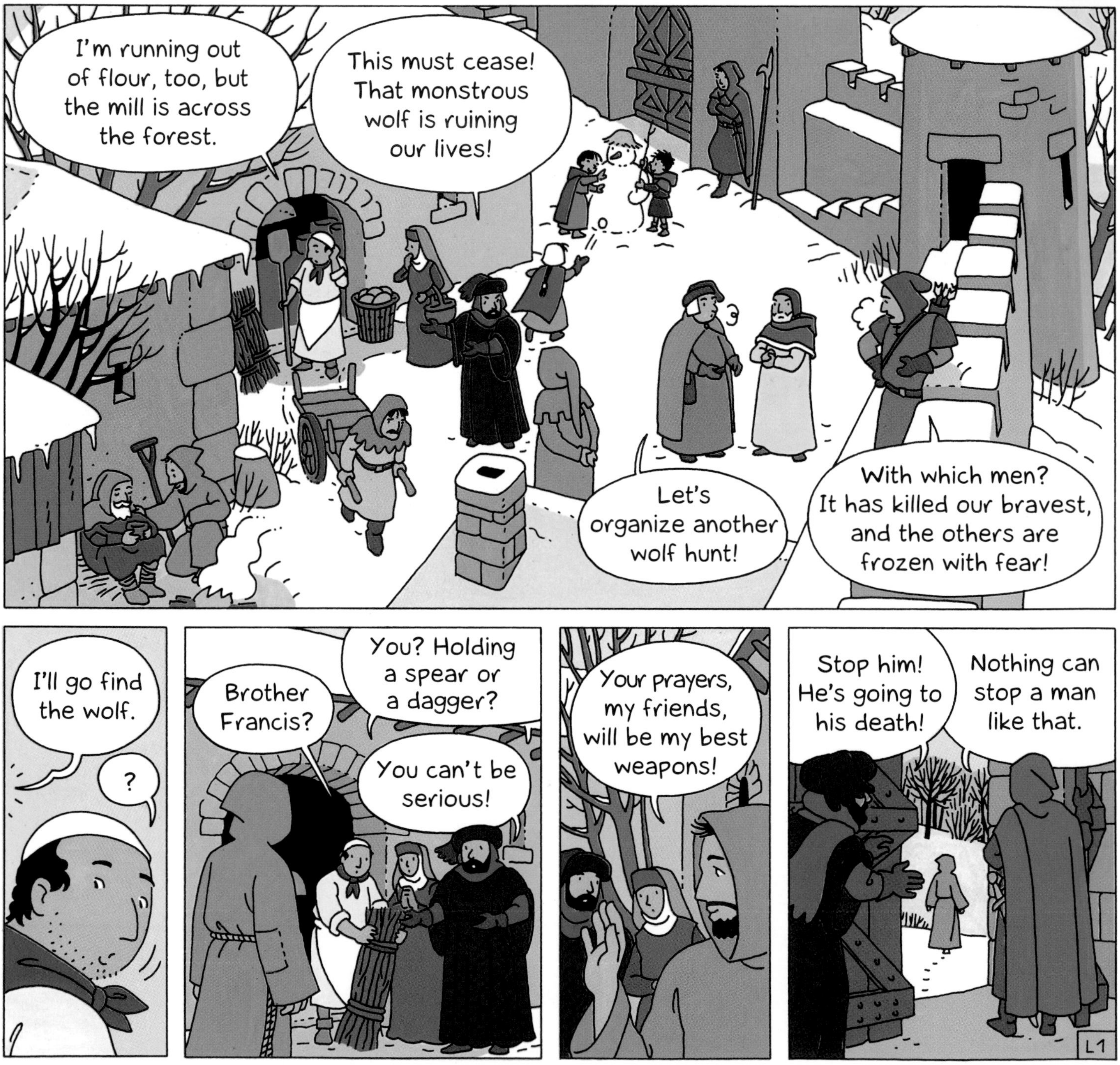
I'm running out of flour, too, but the mill is across the forest.
This must cease! That monstrous wolf is ruining our lives!
Let's organize another wolf hunt!
With which men? It has killed our bravest, and the others are frozen with fear!
I'll go find the wolf.
?
Brother Francis?
You? Holding a spear or a dagger?
You can't be serious!
Your prayers, my friends, will be my best weapons!
Stop him! He's going to his death!
Nothing can stop a man like that.

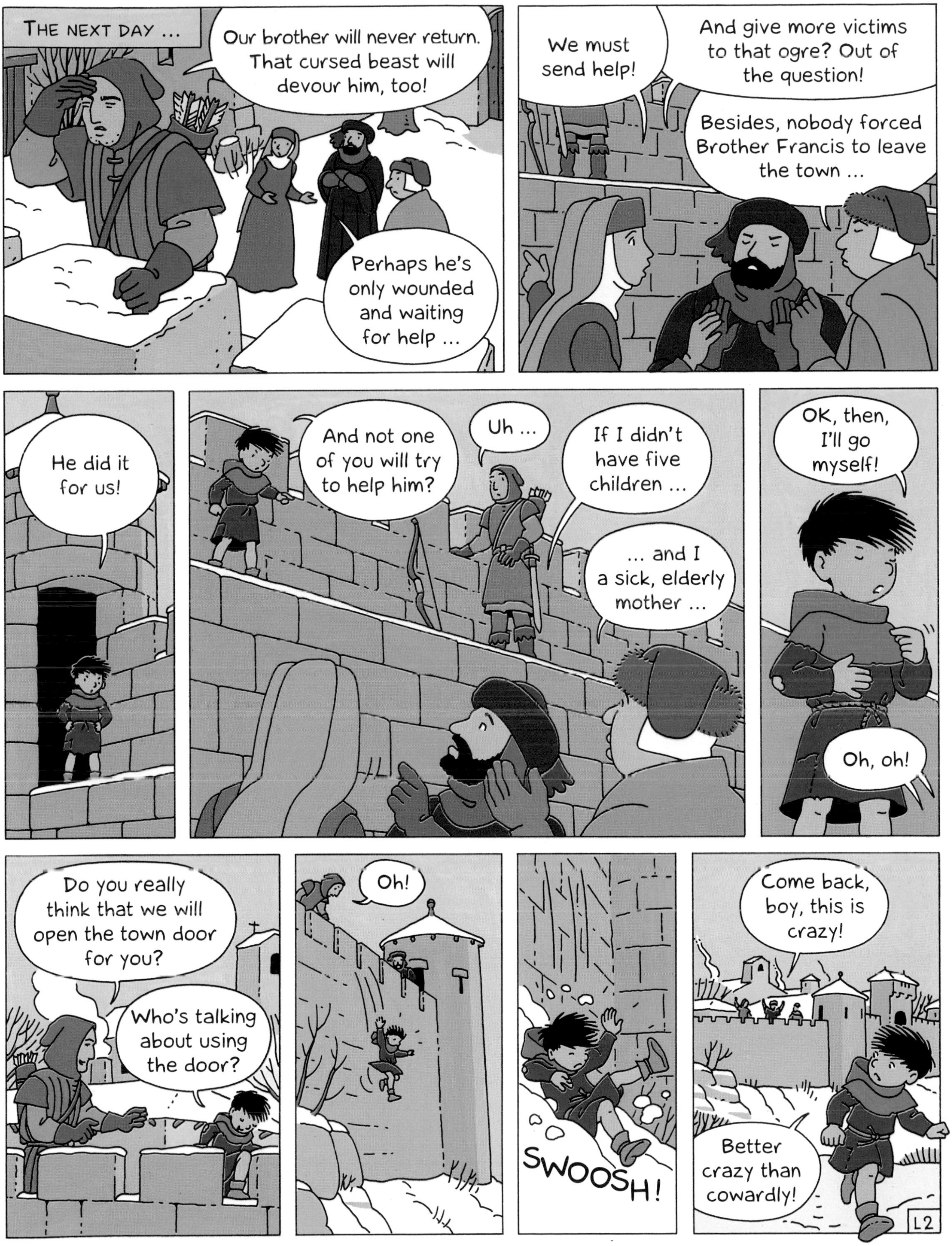
THE NEXT DAY ...
Our brother will never return. That cursed beast will devour him, too!
Perhaps he's only wounded and waiting for help ...
We must send help!
And give more victims to that ogre? Out of the question!
Besides, nobody forced Brother Francis to leave the town ...
He did it for us!
And not one of you will try to help him?
Uh ...
If I didn't have five children ...
... and I a sick, elderly mother ...
OK, then, I'll go myself!
Oh, oh!
Do you really think that we will open the town door for you?
Who's talking about using the door?
Oh!
SWOOSH!
Come back, boy, this is crazy!
Better crazy than cowardly!
L2

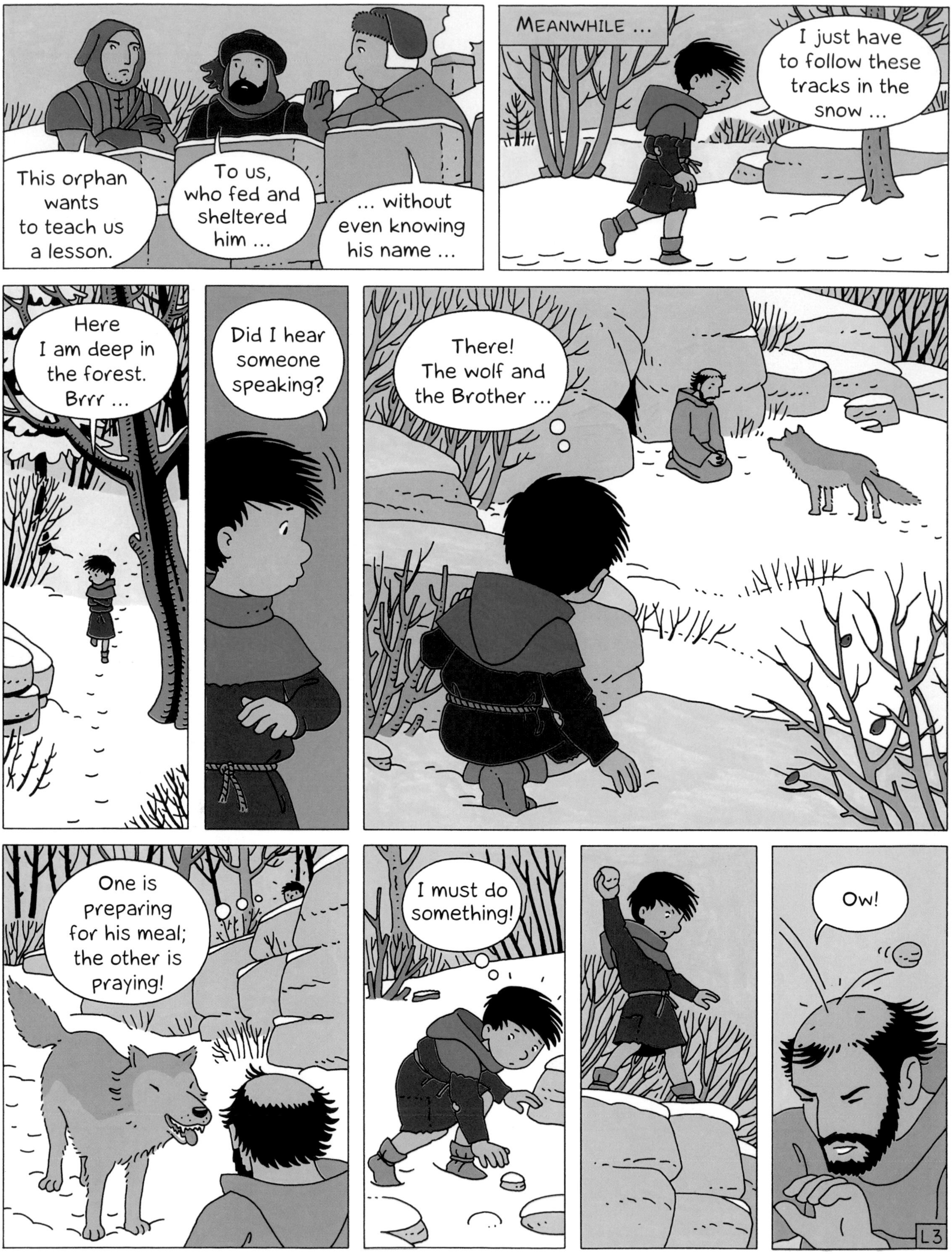
This orphan wants to teach us a lesson.
To us, who fed and sheltered him ...
... without even knowing his name ...
MEANWHILE ...
I just have to follow these tracks in the snow ...
Here I am deep in the forest. Brrr ...
Did I hear someone speaking?
There! The wolf and the Brother ...
One is preparing for his meal; the other is praying!
I must do something!
Ow!
L3

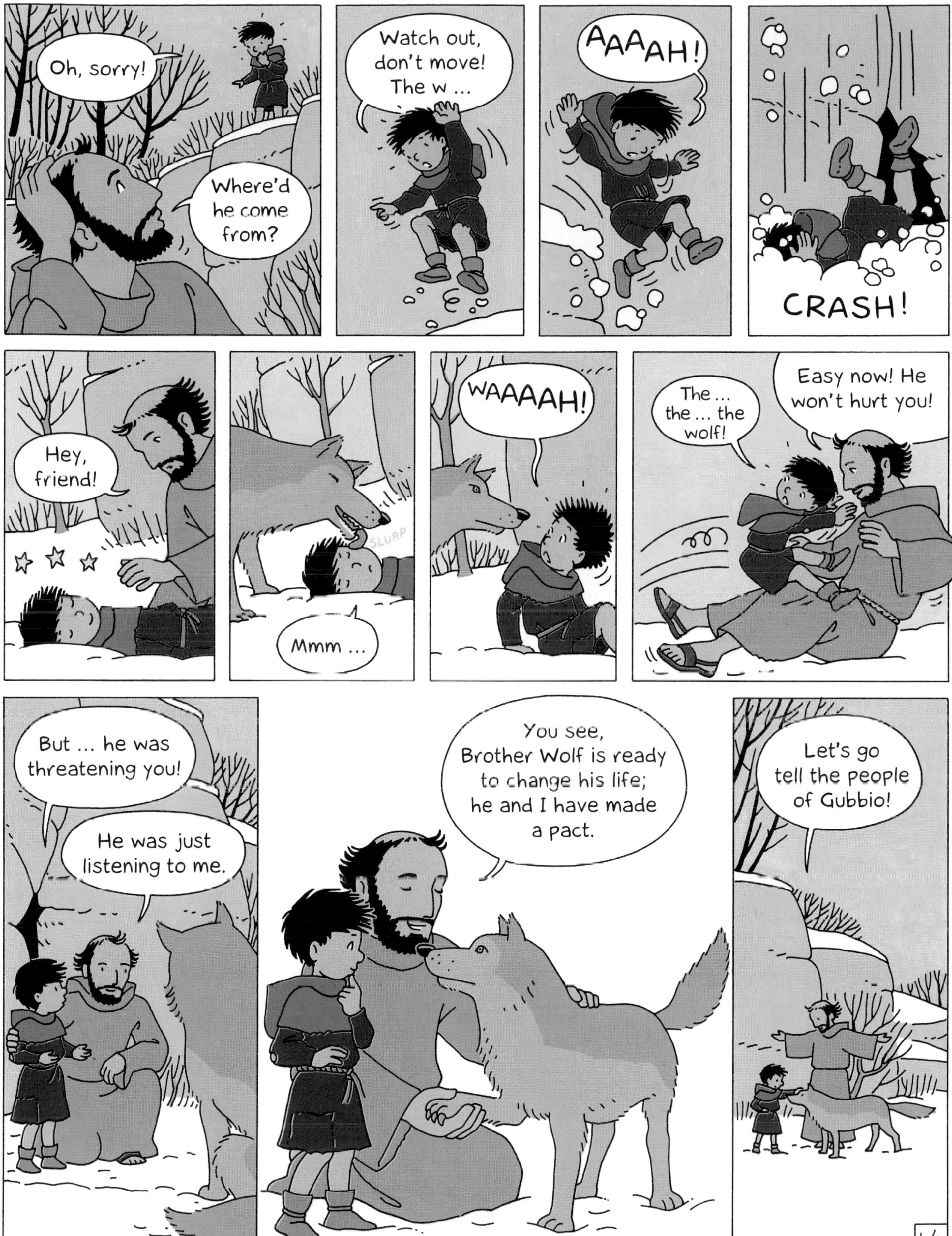

Oh, sorry!
Where'd he come from?
Watch out, don't move! The w ...
AAAAH!
CRASH!
Hey, friend!
SLURP
Mmm ...
WAAAAH!
The ... the ... the wolf!
Easy now! He won't hurt you!
But ... he was threatening you!
He was just listening to me.
You see, Brother Wolf is ready to change his life; he and I have made a pact.
Let's go tell the people of Gubbio!
L4

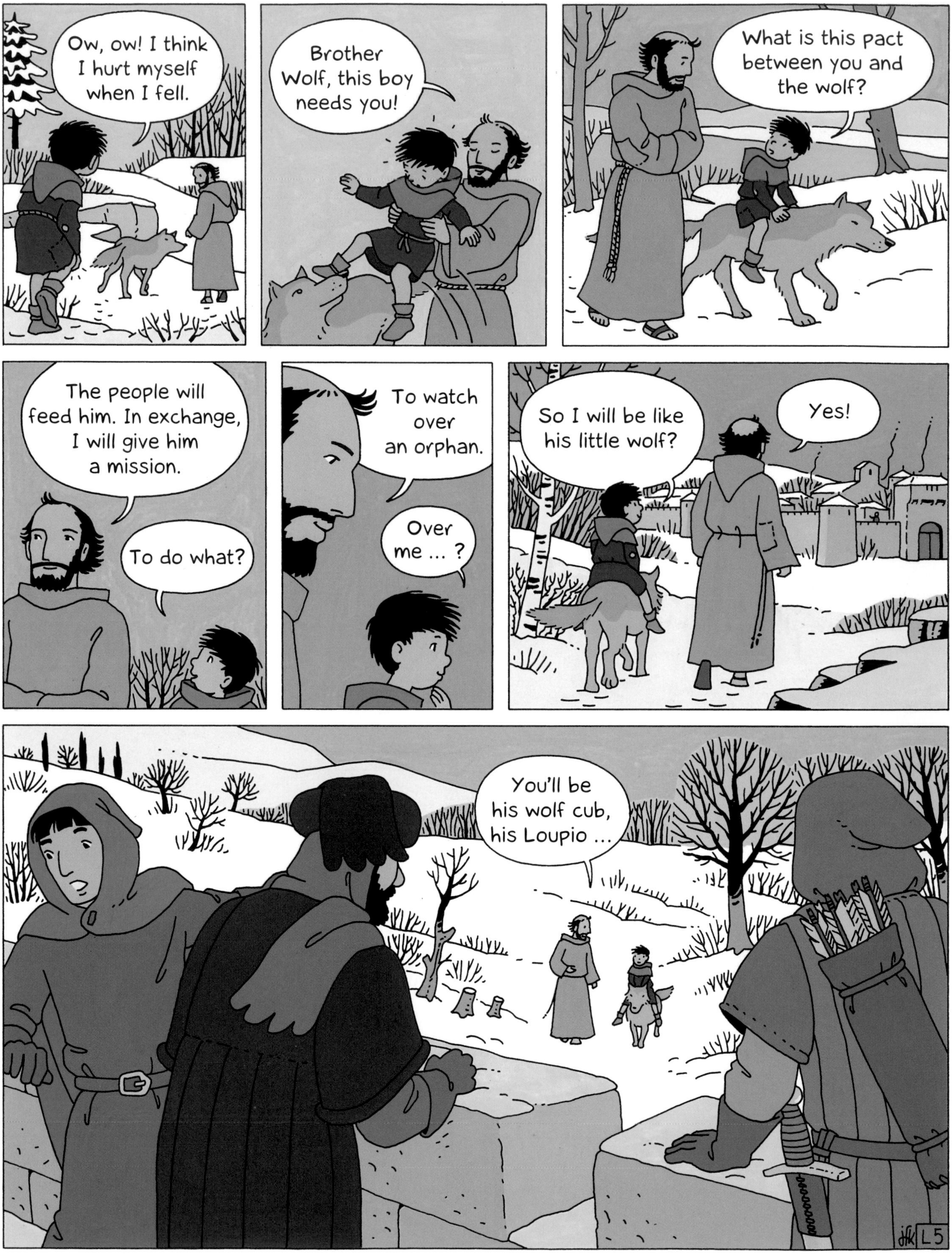

Ow, ow! I think I hurt myself when I fell.
Brother Wolf, this boy needs you!
What is this pact between you and the wolf?
The people will feed him. In exchange, I will give him a mission.
To do what?
To watch over an orphan.
Over me ... ?
So I will be like his little wolf?
Yes!
You'll be his wolf cub, his Loupio ...
L5

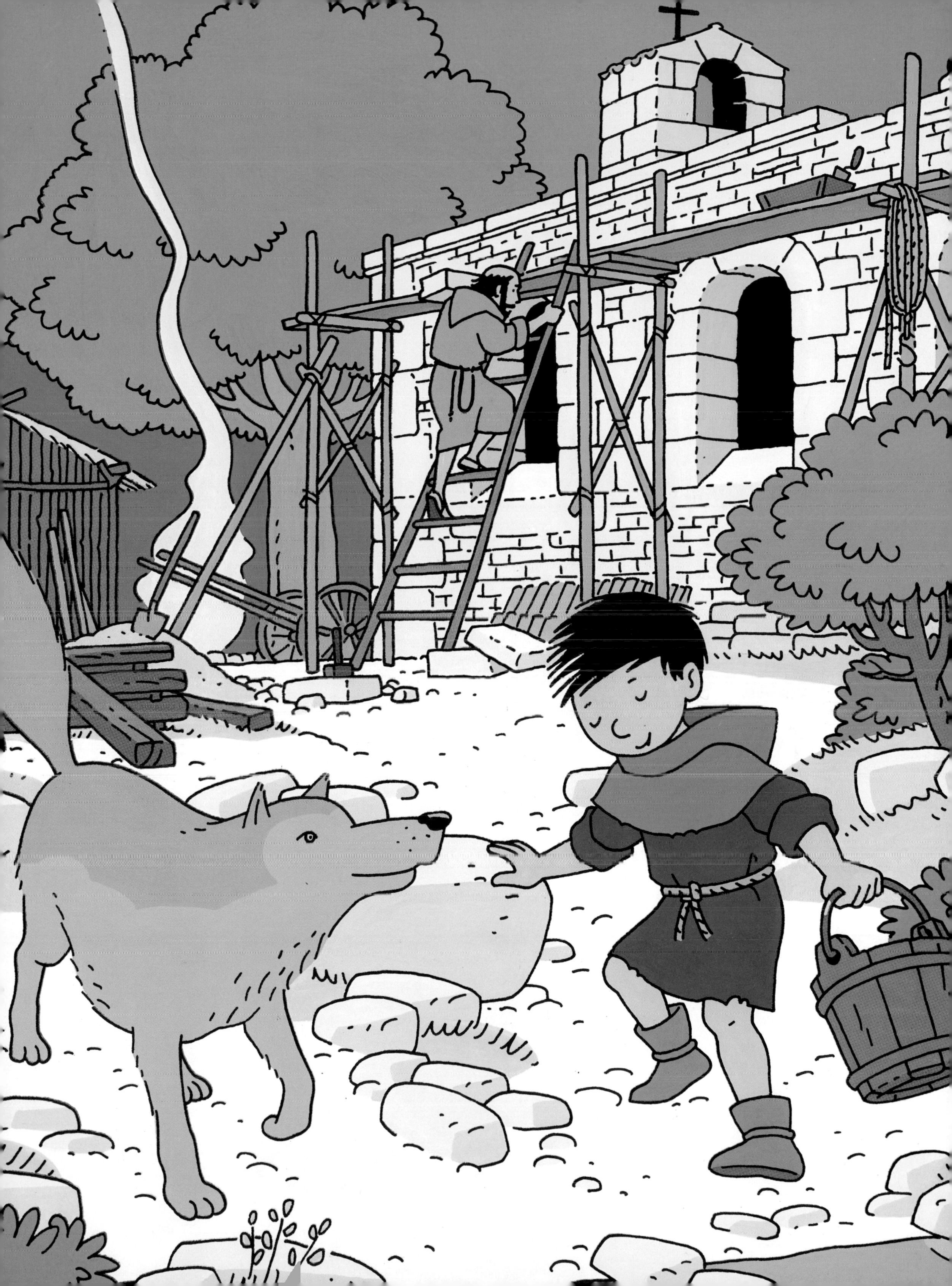

The Cross

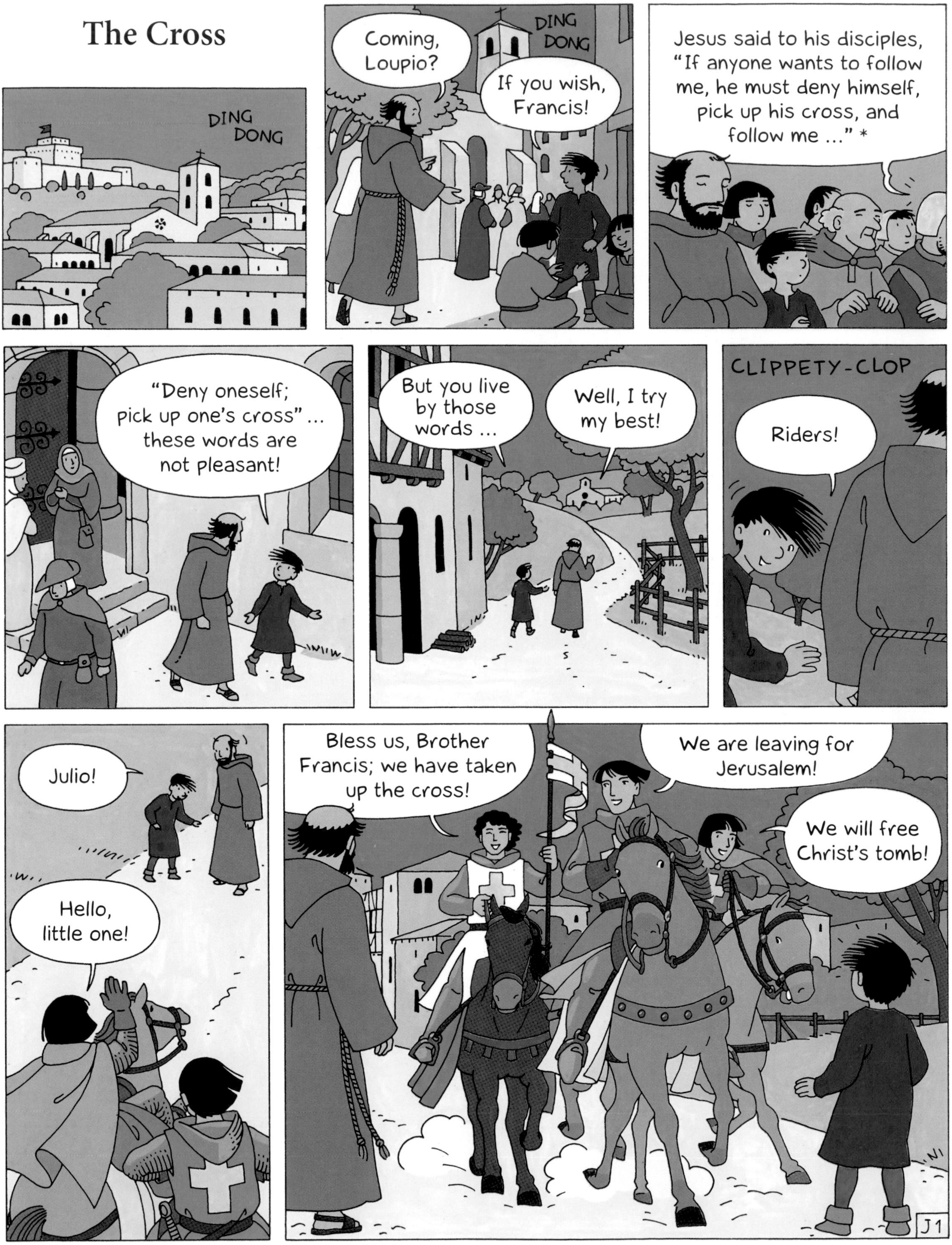
DING DONG
Coming, Loupio?
DING DONG
If you wish, Francis!
Jesus said to his disciples, "If anyone wants to follow me, he must deny himself, pick up his cross, and follow me ..." *
"Deny oneself; pick up one's cross" ... these words are not pleasant!
But you live by those words ...
Well, I try my best!
CLIPPETY-CLOP
Riders!
Julio!
Hello, little one!
Bless us, Brother Francis; we have taken up the cross!
We are leaving for Jerusalem!
We will free Christ's tomb!
J1

*Gospel of Matthew, chapter 16, verse 24

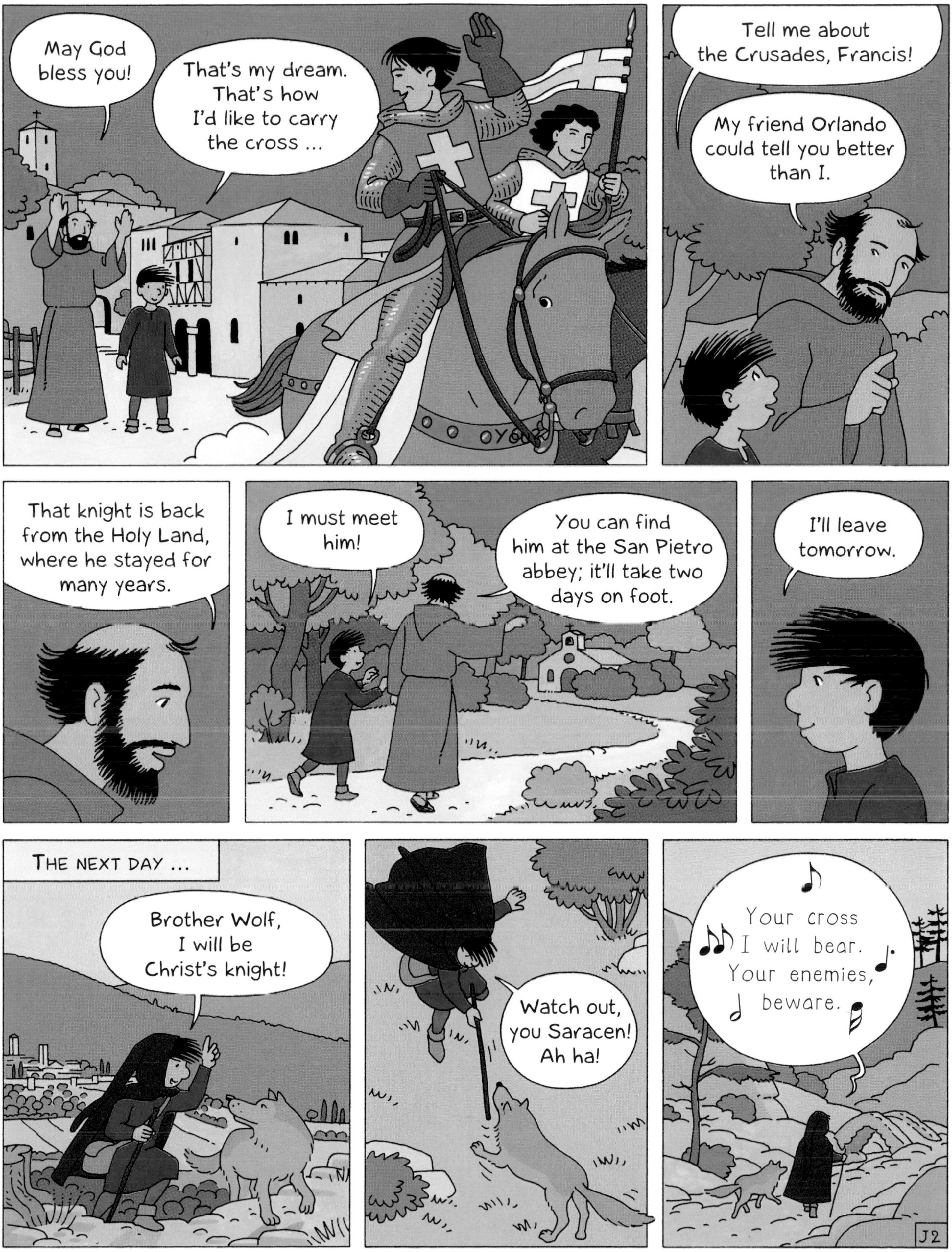
May God bless you!
That's my dream. That's how I'd like to carry the cross ...
Tell me about the Crusades, Francis!
My friend Orlando could tell you better than I.
That knight is back from the Holy Land, where he stayed for many years.
I must meet him!
You can find him at the San Pietro abbey; it'll take two days on foot.
I'll leave tomorrow.
THE NEXT DAY ...
Brother Wolf, I will be Christ's knight!
Watch out, you Saracen! Ah ha!
Your cross I will bear. Your enemies, beware.
J2

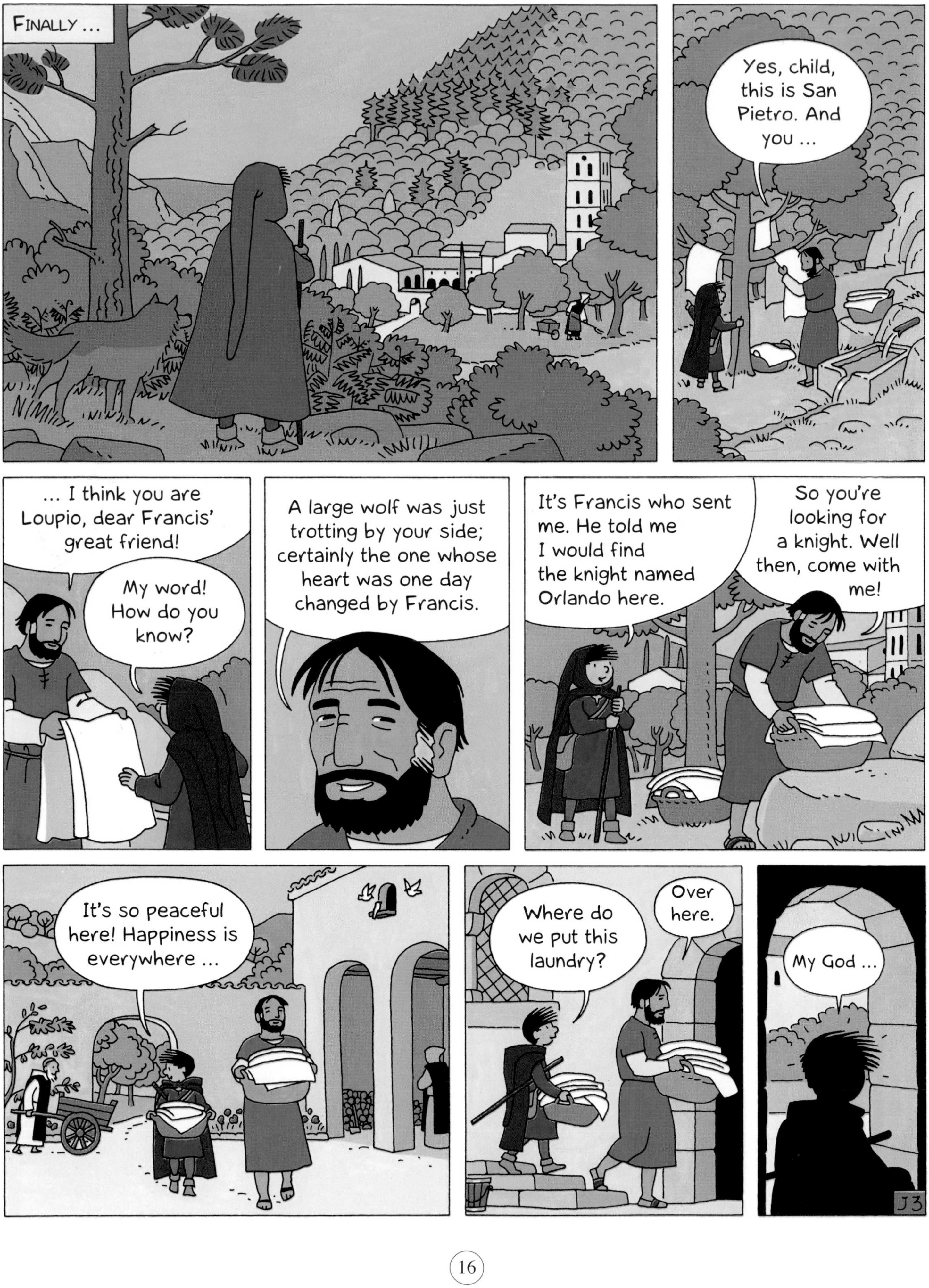
FINALLY ...
Yes, child, this is San Pietro. And you ...
... I think you are Loupio, dear Francis' great friend!
My word! How do you know?
A large wolf was just trotting by your side; certainly the one whose heart was one day changed by Francis.
It's Francis who sent me. He told me I would find the knight named Orlando here.
So you're looking for a knight. Well then, come with me!
It's so peaceful here! Happiness is everywhere ...
Where do we put this laundry?
Over here.
My God ...
J3

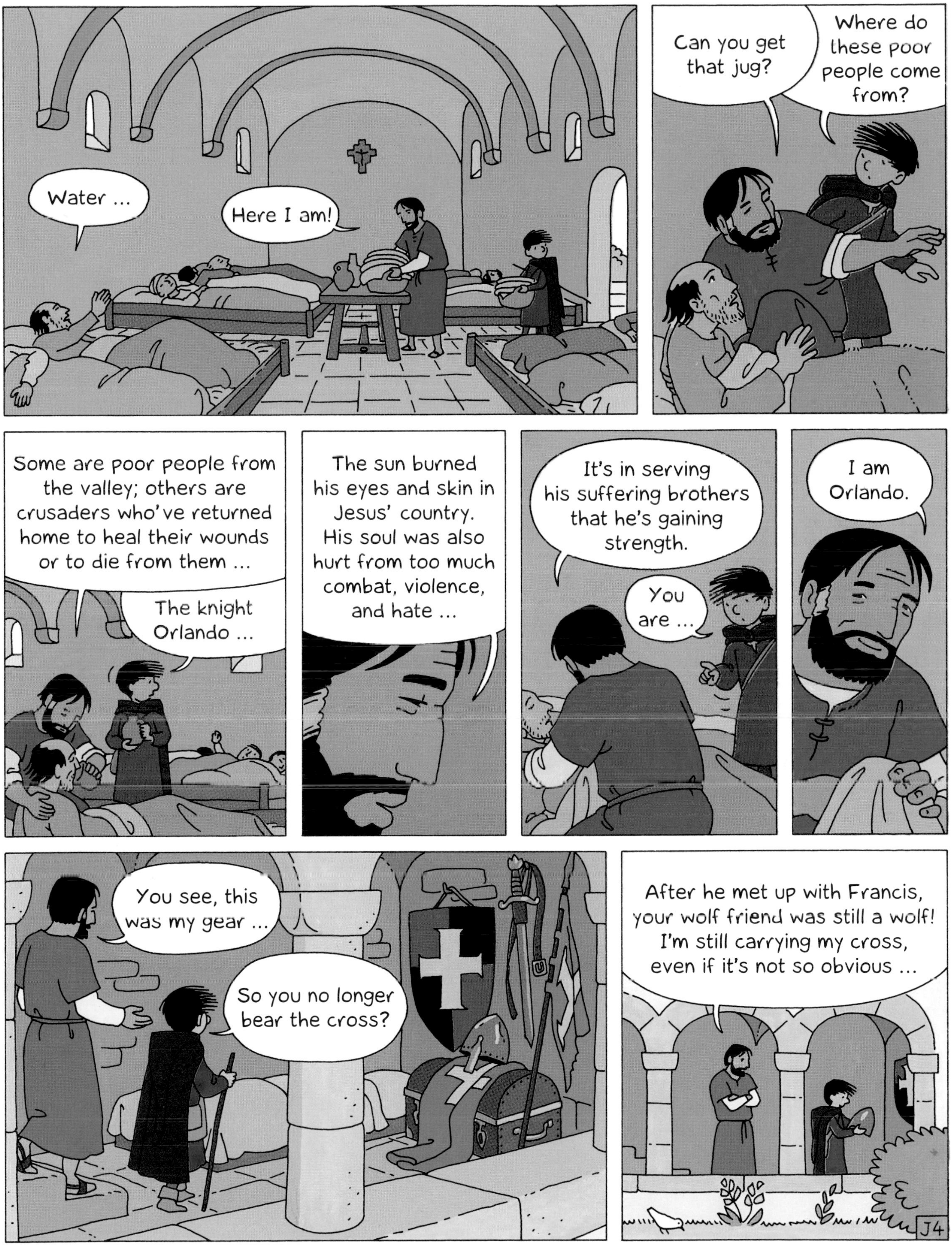
Water ...
Here I am!
Can you get that jug?
Where do these poor people come from?
Some are poor people from the valley; others are crusaders who've returned home to heal their wounds or to die from them ...
The knight Orlando ...
The sun burned his eyes and skin in Jesus' country. His soul was also hurt from too much combat, violence, and hate ...
It's in serving his suffering brothers that he's gaining strength.
You are ...
I am Orlando.
You see, this was my gear ...
So you no longer bear the cross?
After he met up with Francis, your wolf friend was still a wolf! I'm still carrying my cross, even if it's not so obvious ...
J4

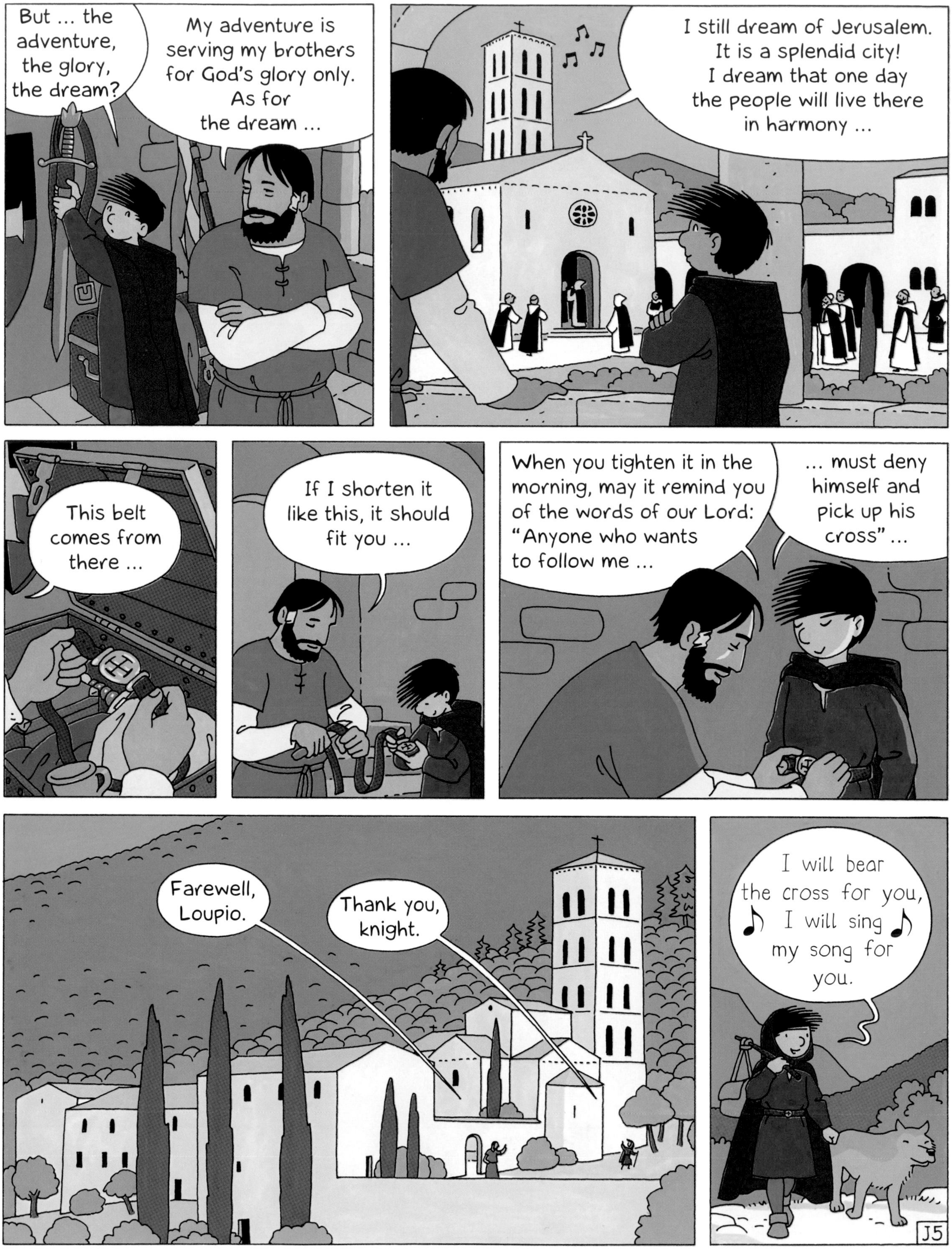
But ... the adventure, the glory, the dream?
My adventure is serving my brothers for God's glory only. As for the dream ...
I still dream of Jerusalem. It is a splendid city! I dream that one day the people will live there in harmony ...
This belt comes from there ...
If I shorten it like this, it should fit you ...
When you tighten it in the morning, may it remind you of the words of our Lord: "Anyone who wants to follow me ...
... must deny himself and pick up his cross" ...
Farewell, Loupio.
Thank you, knight.
I will bear the cross for you, I will sing my song for you.
J5

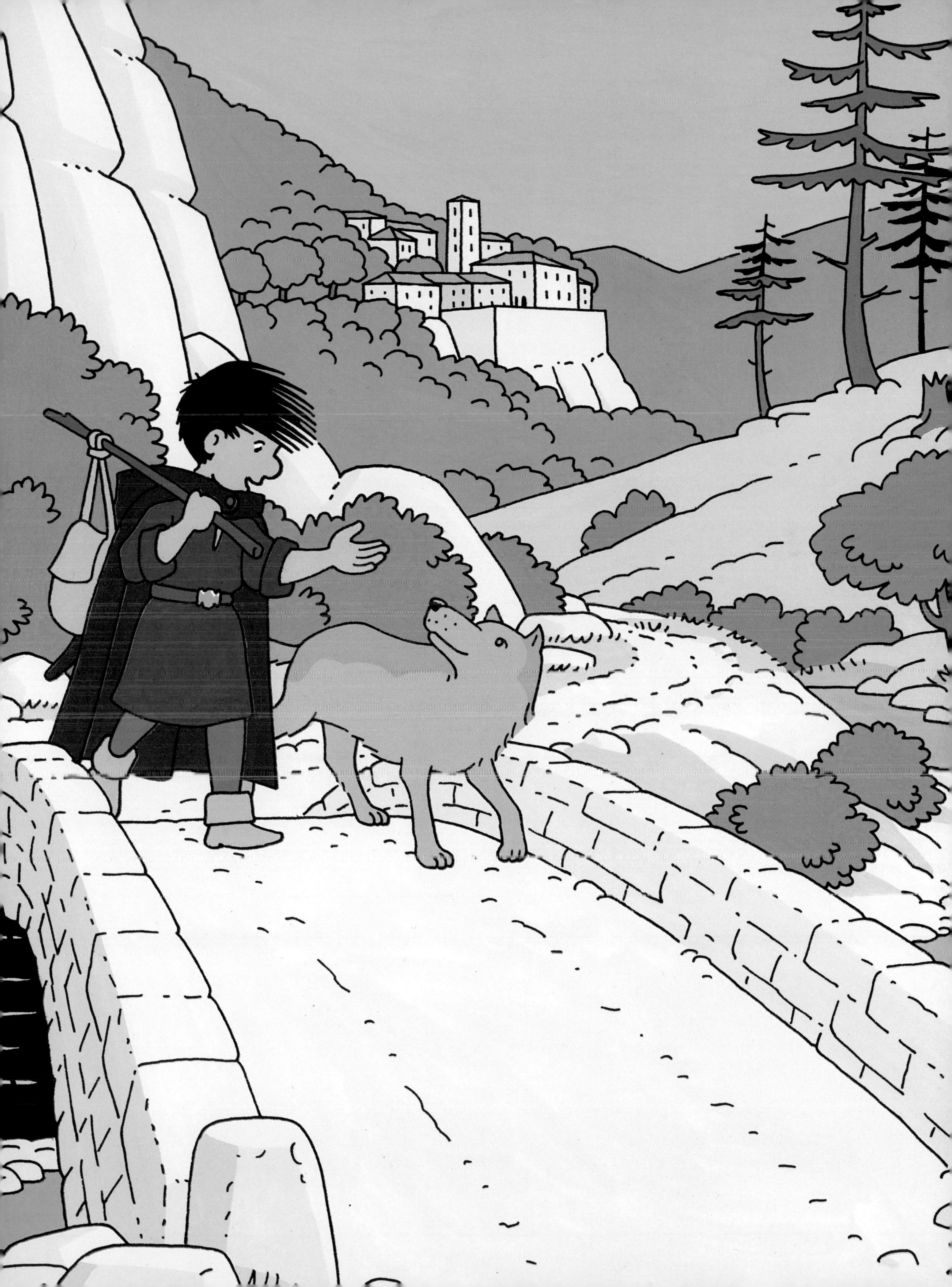

The Lute

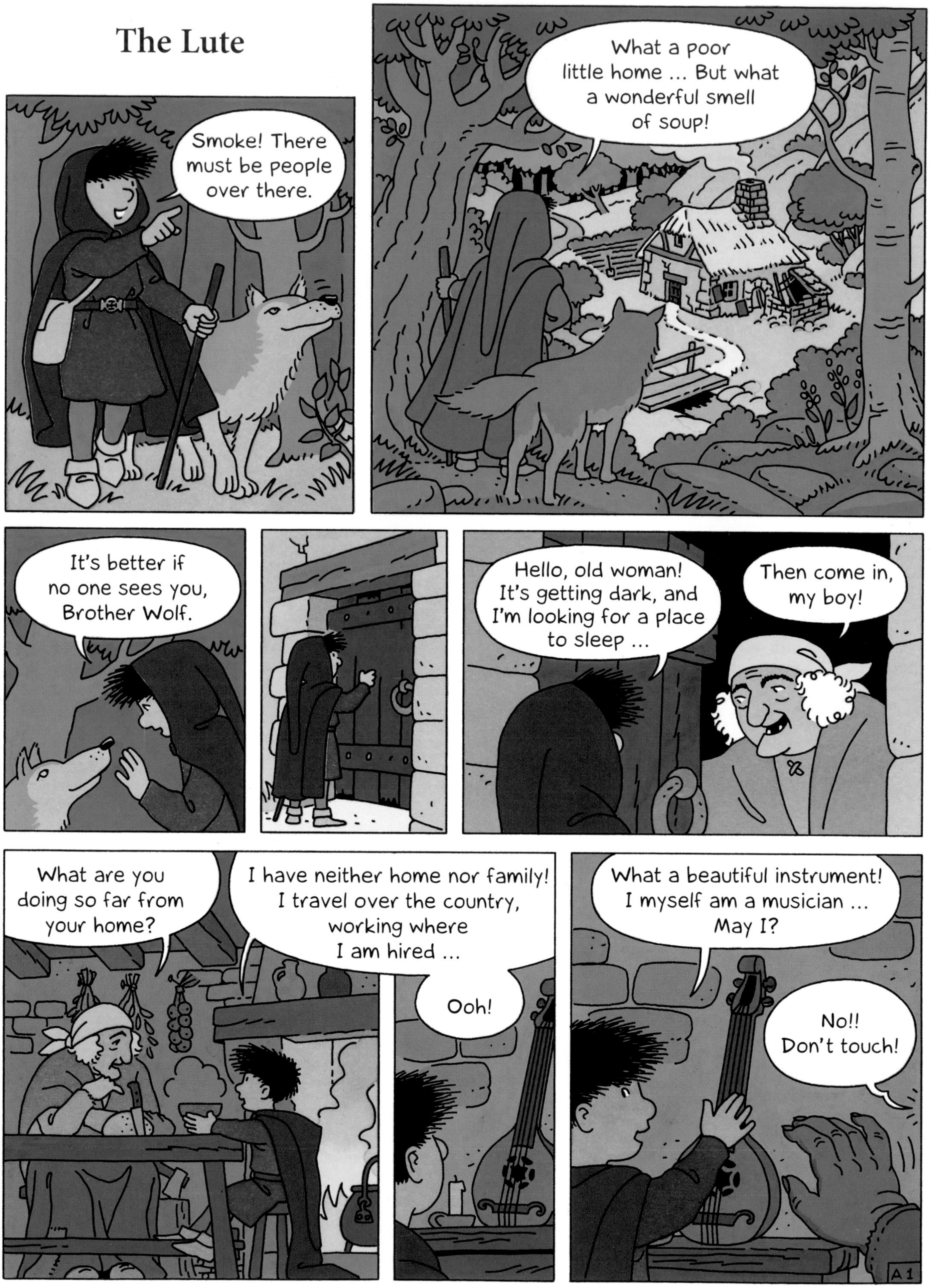
Smoke! There must be people over there.
What a poor little home ... But what a wonderful smell of soup!
It's better if no one sees you, Brother Wolf.
Hello, old woman! It's getting dark, and I'm looking for a place to sleep ...
Then come in, my boy!
What are you doing so far from your home?
I have neither home nor family! I travel over the country, working where I am hired ...
Ooh!
What a beautiful instrument! I myself am a musician ... May I?
No!! Don't touch!
A 1

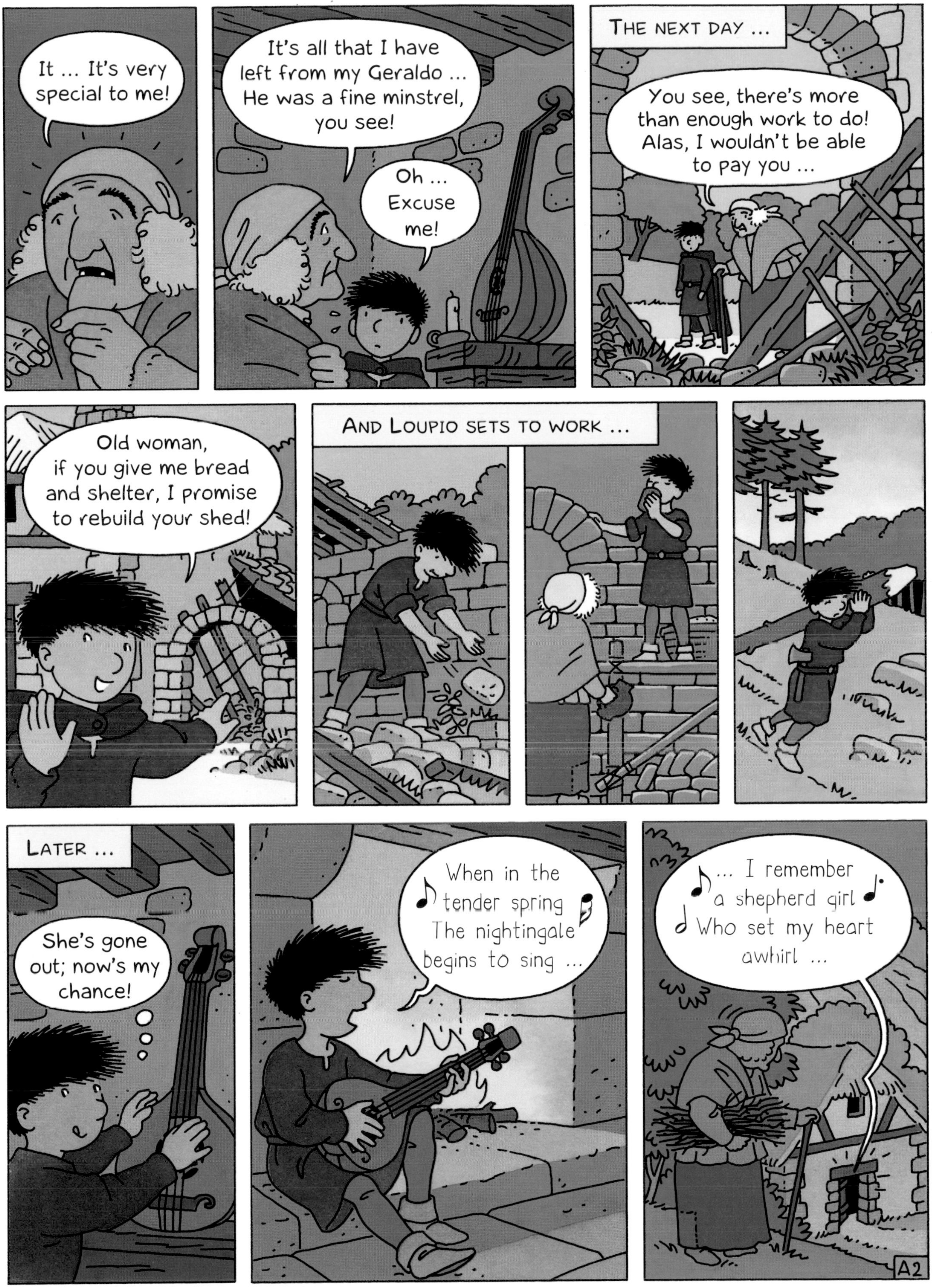
It ... It's very special to me!
It's all that I have left from my Geraldo ... He was a fine minstrel, you see!
Oh ... Excuse me!
THE NEXT DAY ...
You see, there's more than enough work to do! Alas, I wouldn't be able to pay you ...
Old woman, if you give me bread and shelter, I promise to rebuild your shed!
AND LOUPIO SETS TO WORK ...
LATER ...
She's gone out; now's my chance!
When in the tender spring The nightingale begins to sing ...
... I remember a shepherd girl Who set my heart awhirl ...
A2

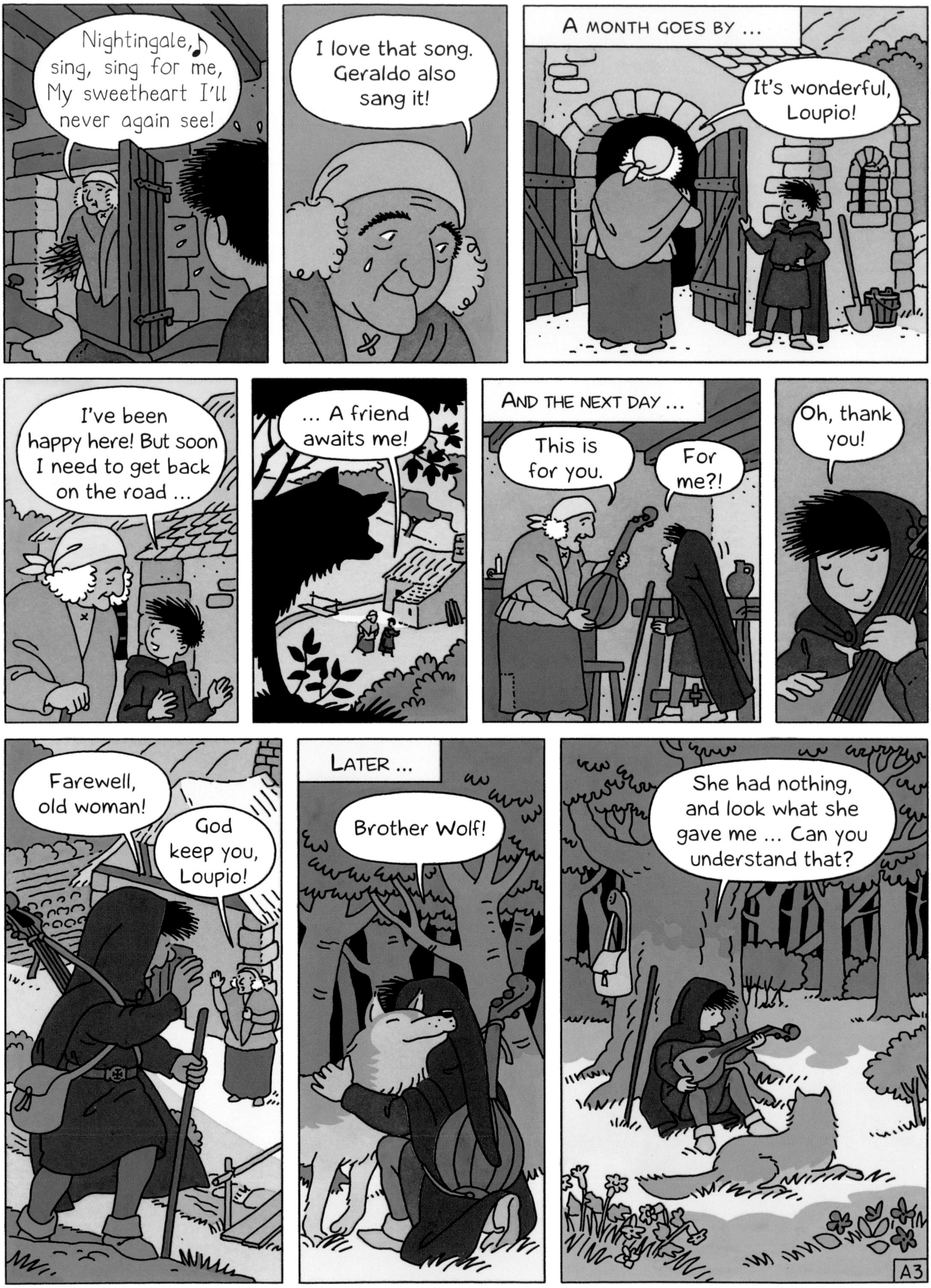
Nightingale, sing, sing for me, My sweetheart I'll never again see!
I love that song. Geraldo also sang it!
A MONTH GOES BY ...
It's wonderful, Loupio!
I've been happy here! But soon I need to get back on the road ...
... A friend awaits me!
AND THE NEXT DAY ...
This is for you.
For me?!
Oh, thank you!
Farewell, old woman!
God keep you, Loupio!
LATER ...
Brother Wolf!
She had nothing, and look what she gave me ... Can you understand that?
A3

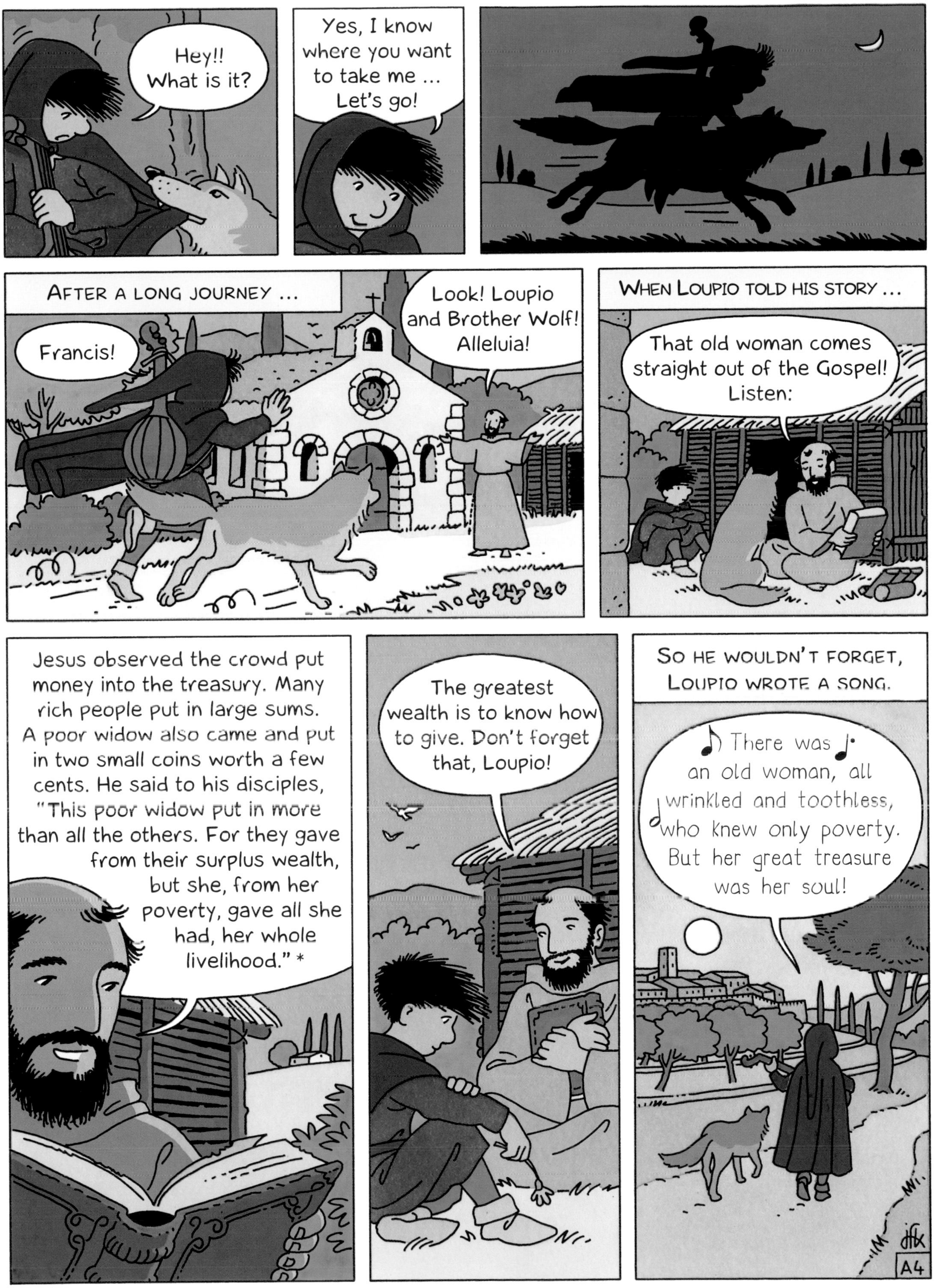
Hey!! What is it?
Yes, I know where you want to take me ... Let's go!
AFTER A LONG JOURNEY ...
Francis!
Look! Loupio and Brother Wolf! Alleluia!
WHEN LOUPIO TOLD HIS STORY ...
That old woman comes straight out of the Gospel! Listen:
Jesus observed the crowd put money into the treasury. Many rich people put in large sums. A poor widow also came and put in two small coins worth a few cents. He said to his disciples, "This poor widow put in more than all the others. For they gave from their surplus wealth, but she, from her poverty, gave all she had, her whole livelihood." *
The greatest wealth is to know how to give. Don't forget that, Loupio!
SO HE WOULDN'T FORGET, LOUPIO WROTE A SONG.
There was an old woman, all wrinkled and toothless, who knew only poverty. But her great treasure was her soul!
A4

*Gospel of Mark, chapter 12, verses 41 to 44

The Rivals

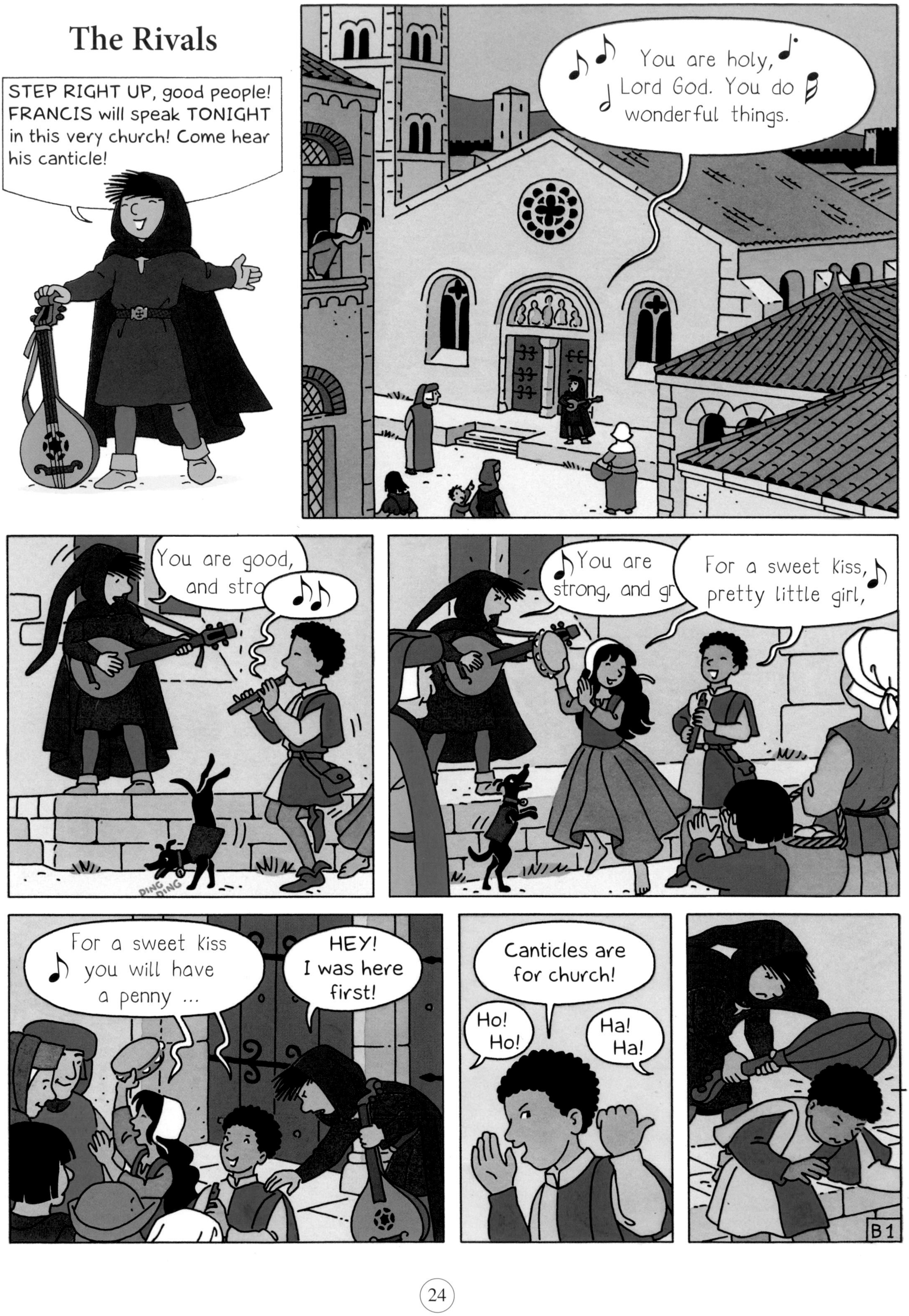
STEP RIGHT UP, good people! FRANCIS will speak TONIGHT in this very church! Come hear his canticle!
You are holy, Lord God. You do wonderful things.
You are good, and stro
You are strong, and gr
For a sweet kiss, pretty little girl,
PING DING
For a sweet kiss you will have a penny ...
HEY! I was here first!
Canticles are for church!
Ho! Ho!
Ha! Ha!
B1

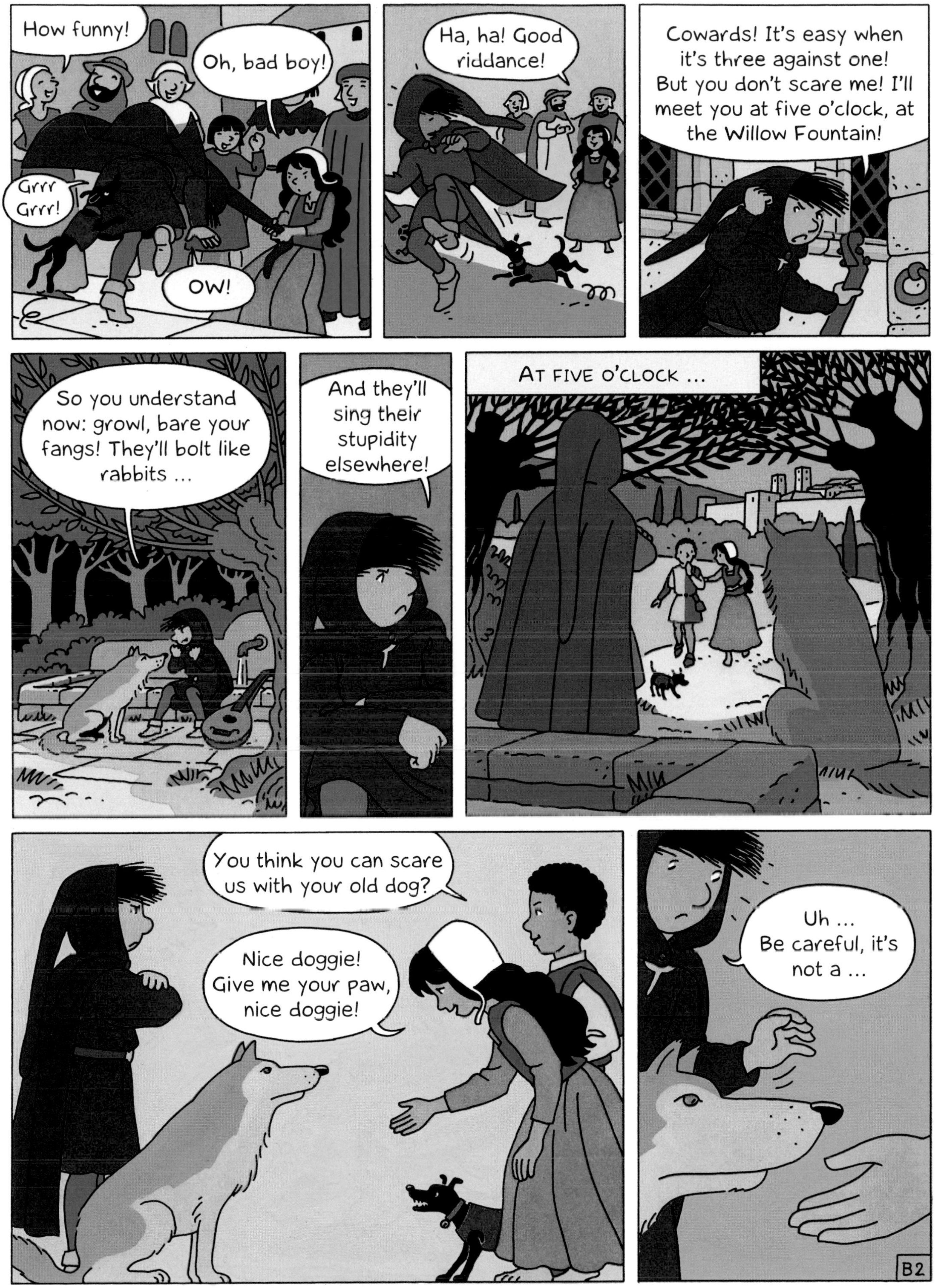
How funny!
Oh, bad boy!
Grrr Grrr!
OW!
Ha, ha! Good riddance!
Cowards! It's easy when it's three against one! But you don't scare me! I'll meet you at five o'clock, at the Willow Fountain!
So you understand now: growl, bare your fangs! They'll bolt like rabbits ...
And they'll sing their stupidity elsewhere!
AT FIVE O'CLOCK ...
You think you can scare us with your old dog?
Nice doggie! Give me your paw, nice doggie!
Uh ... Be careful, it's not a ...
B2

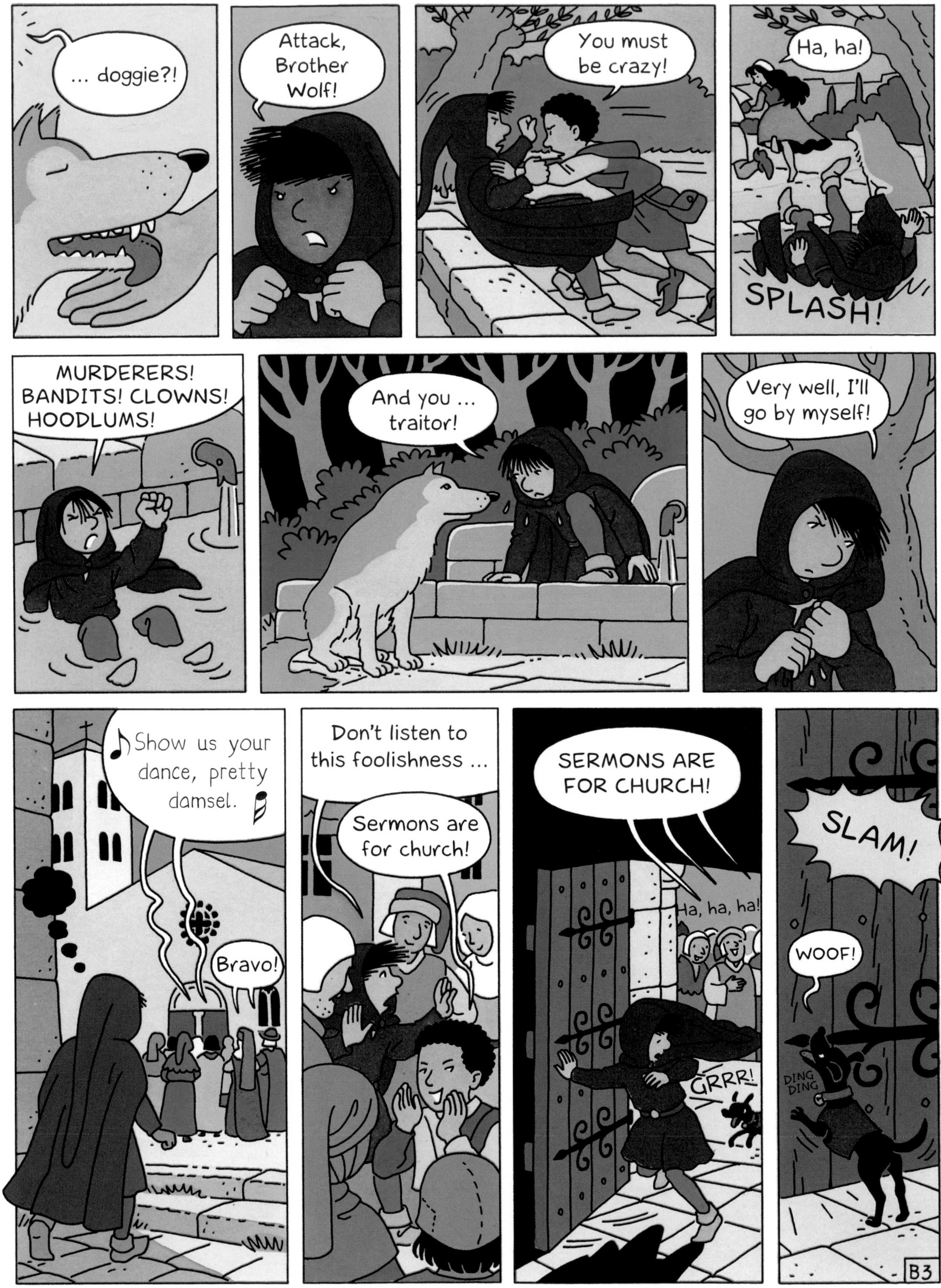
... doggie?!
Attack, Brother Wolf!
You must be crazy!
Ha, ha!
SPLASH!
MURDERERS! BANDITS! CLOWNS! HOODLUMS!
And you ... traitor!
Very well, I'll go by myself!
Show us your dance, pretty damsel.
Bravo!
Don't listen to this foolishness ...
Sermons are for church!
SERMONS ARE FOR CHURCH!
Ha, ha, ha!
GRRR!
SLAM!
WOOF!
DING DING
B3

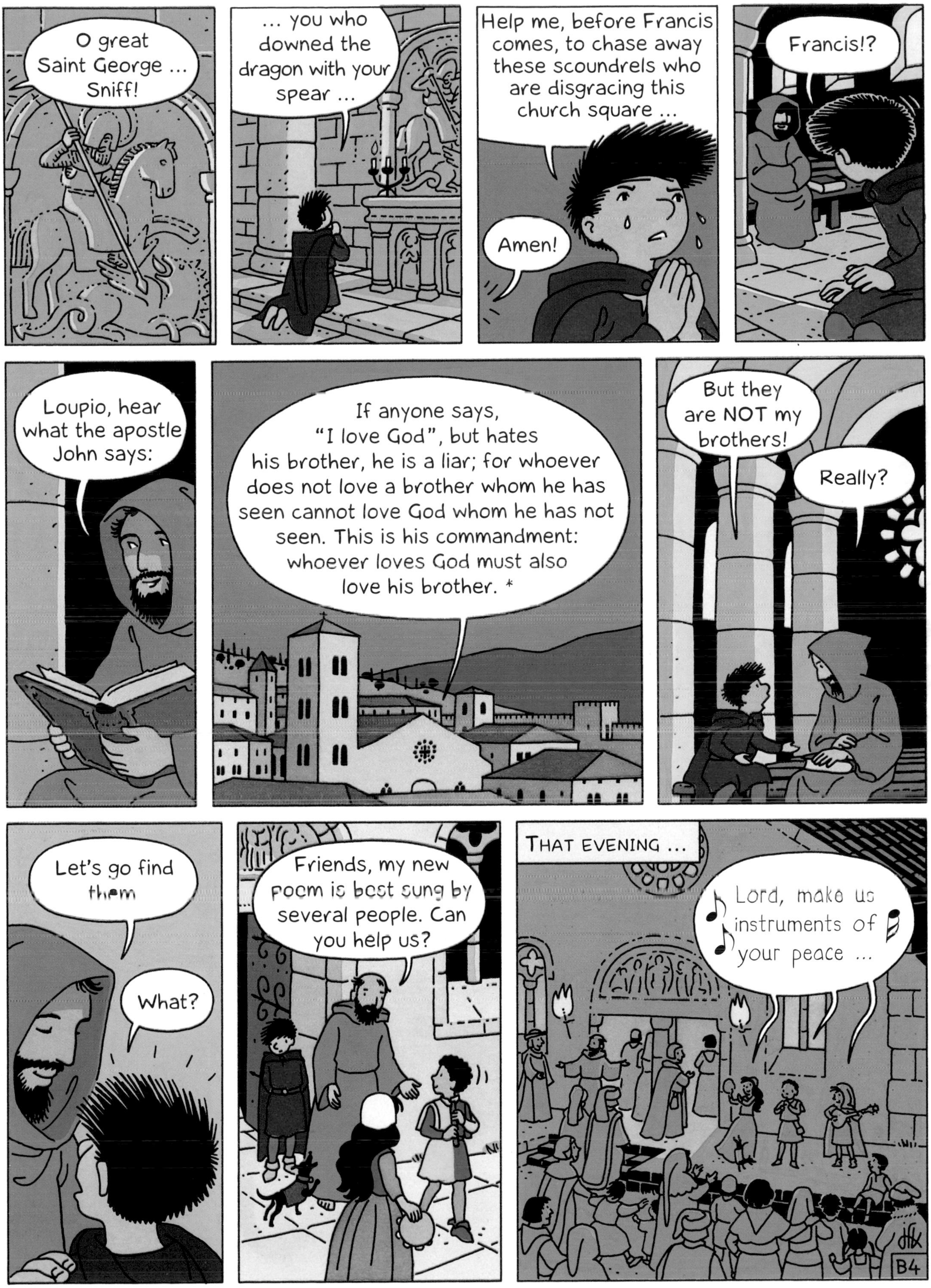
O great Saint George ... Sniff!
... you who downed the dragon with your spear ...
Help me, before Francis comes, to chase away these scoundrels who are disgracing this church square ...
Amen!
Francis!?
Loupio, hear what the apostle John says:
If anyone says, "I love God", but hates his brother, he is a liar; for whoever does not love a brother whom he has seen cannot love God whom he has not seen. This is his commandment: whoever loves God must also love his brother. *
But they are NOT my brothers!
Really?
Let's go find them
What?
Friends, my new poem is best sung by several people. Can you help us?
THAT EVENING ...
Lord, make us instruments of your peace ...

*First Letter of John, chapter 4, verses 20 and 21

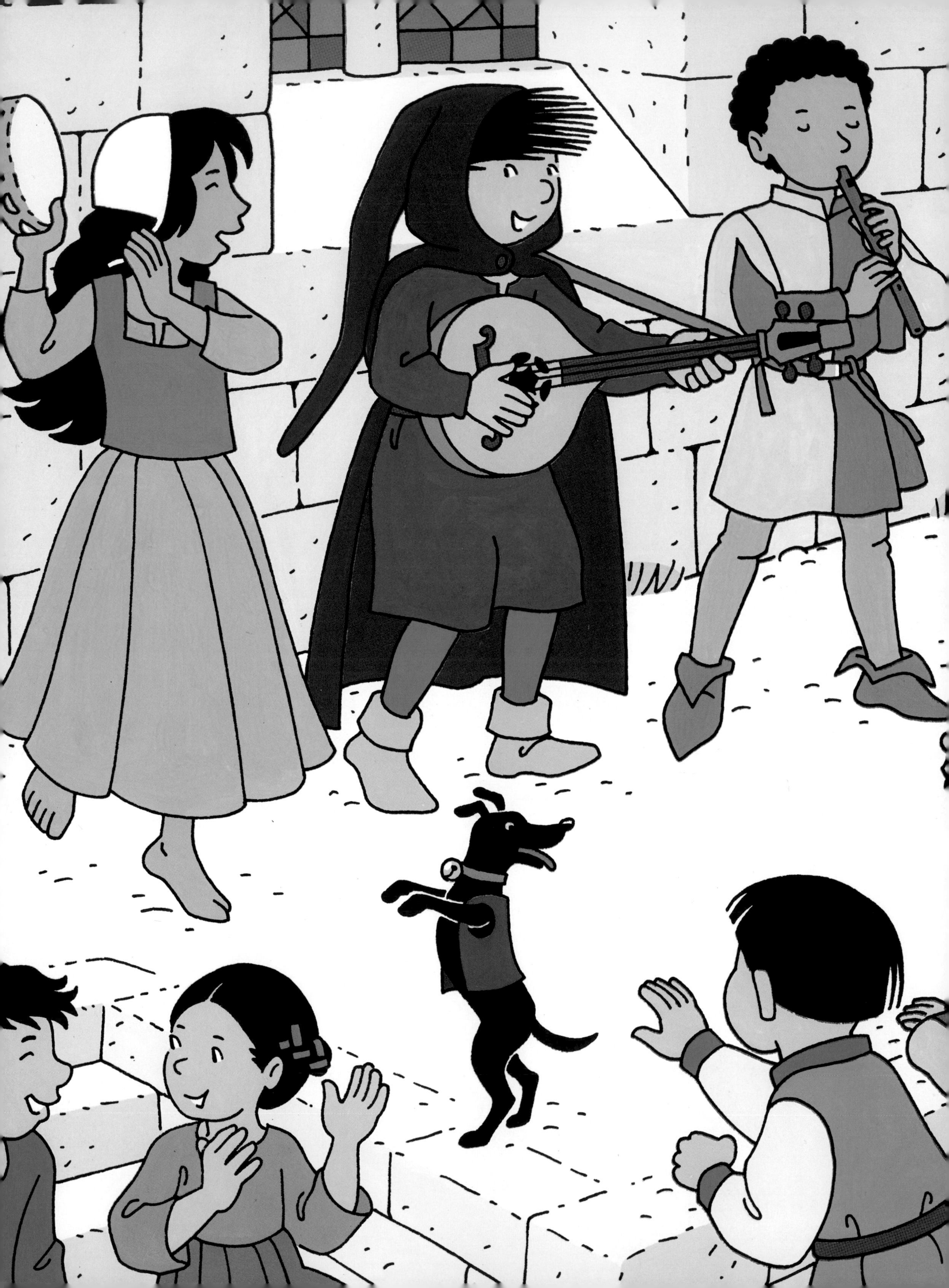

Loupio's Ballad

SOLOIST:
F C Dm
Who is that walk-ing on the way?
ALL:
F C Dm
Who is that walk-ing on the way?
SOLOIST:
Dm C Dm Am
It's lit - tle Lou-pio sing - ing songs.
ALL:
Dm C Dm C Dm
It's lit - tle Lou-pio sing - ing songs.

Who is that walking on the way? (repeat)
It's little Loupio singing songs. (repeat)

By night or day, he never fears. (repeat)
He has a wolf who is his friend. (repeat)

He sings to earn his daily bread. (repeat)
All by himself, he writes his songs. (repeat)

He sings the stories of our lives. (repeat)
He sings our joys and our sorrows. (repeat)

Just like Saint Francis, his dear friend, (repeat)
He sings to God his songs of praise. (repeat)

He's like a pilgrim on his way, (repeat)
Walking to God, day after day. (repeat)

The Beggar

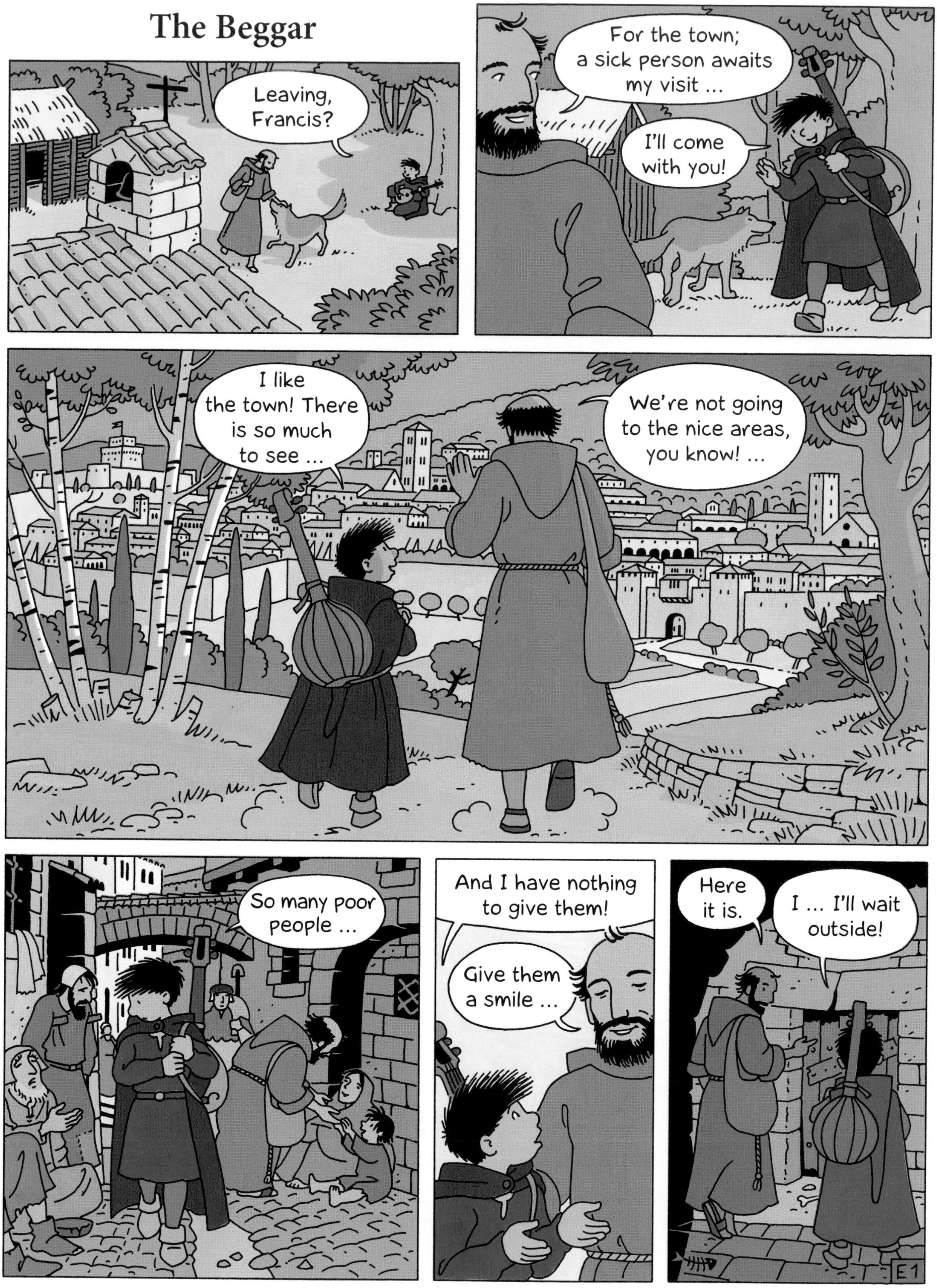

Leaving, Francis?
For the town; a sick person awaits my visit ...
I'll come with you!
I like the town! There is so much to see ...
We're not going to the nice areas, you know! ...
So many poor people ...
And I have nothing to give them!
Give them a smile ...
Here it is.
I ... I'll wait outside!
E1

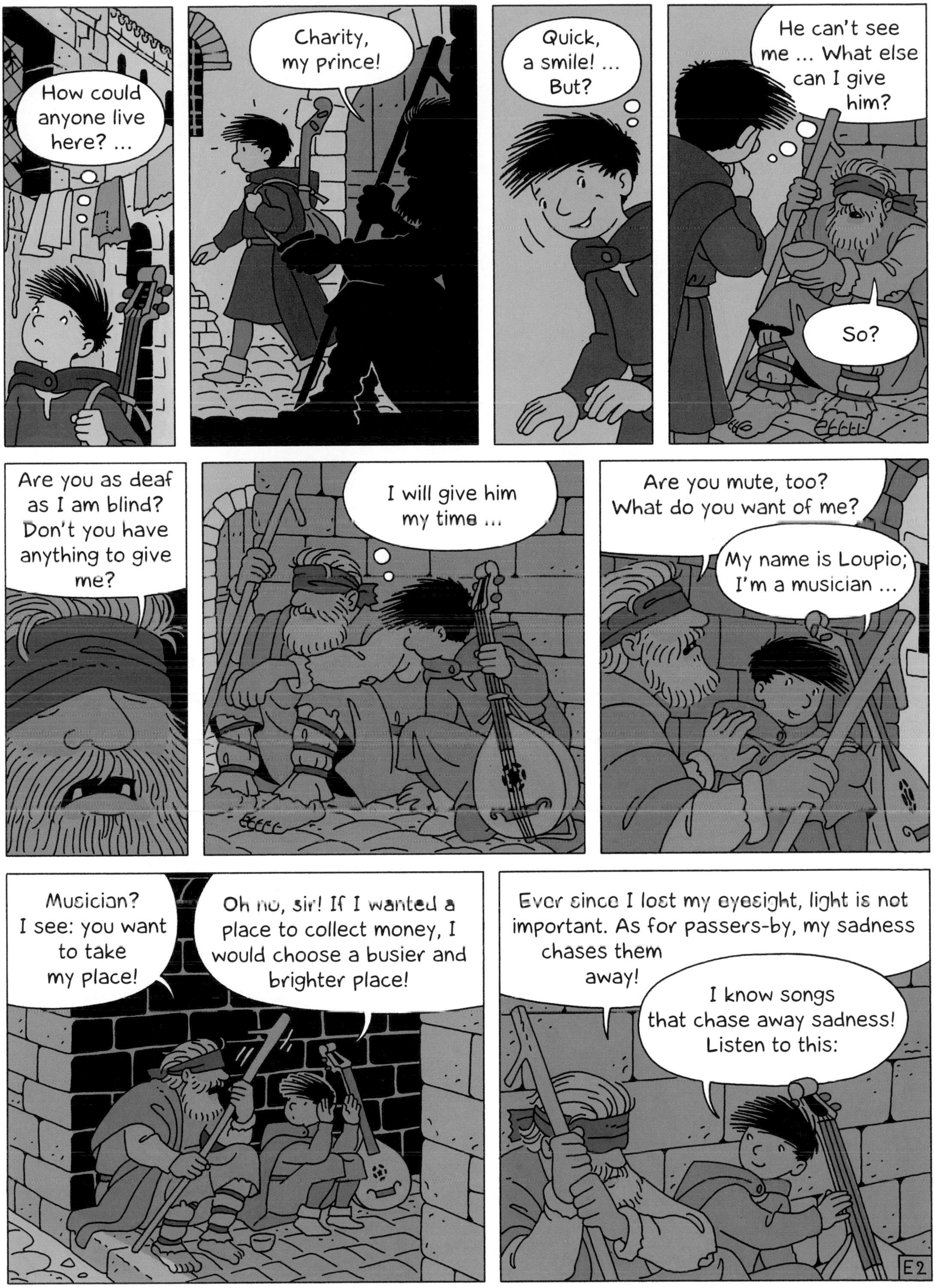
How could anyone live here? ...
Charity, my prince!
Quick, a smile! ... But?
He can't see me ... What else can I give him?
So?
Are you as deaf as I am blind? Don't you have anything to give me?
I will give him my time ...
Are you mute, too? What do you want of me?
My name is Loupio; I'm a musician ...
Musician? I see: you want to take my place!
Oh no, sir! If I wanted a place to collect money, I would choose a busier and brighter place!
Ever since I lost my eyesight, light is not important. As for passers-by, my sadness chases them away!
I know songs that chase away sadness! Listen to this:
E2

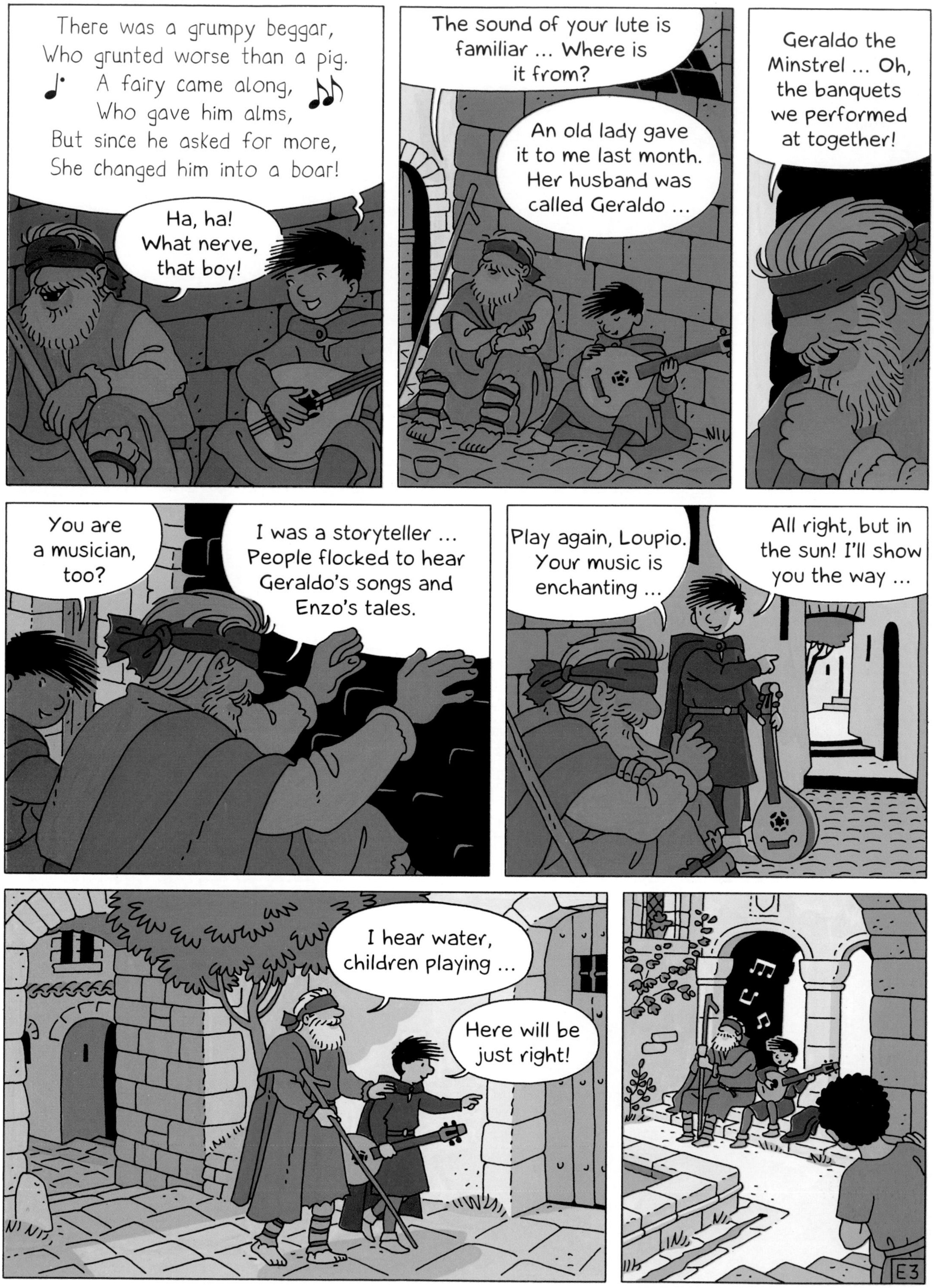
There was a grumpy beggar, Who grunted worse than a pig. A fairy came along, Who gave him alms, But since he asked for more, She changed him into a boar!
Ha, ha! What nerve, that boy!
The sound of your lute is familiar ... Where is it from?
An old lady gave it to me last month. Her husband was called Geraldo ...
Geraldo the Minstrel ... Oh, the banquets we performed at together!
You are a musician, too?
I was a storyteller ... People flocked to hear Geraldo's songs and Enzo's tales.
Play again, Loupio. Your music is enchanting ...
All right, but in the sun! I'll show you the way ...
I hear water, children playing ...
Here will be just right!
E3

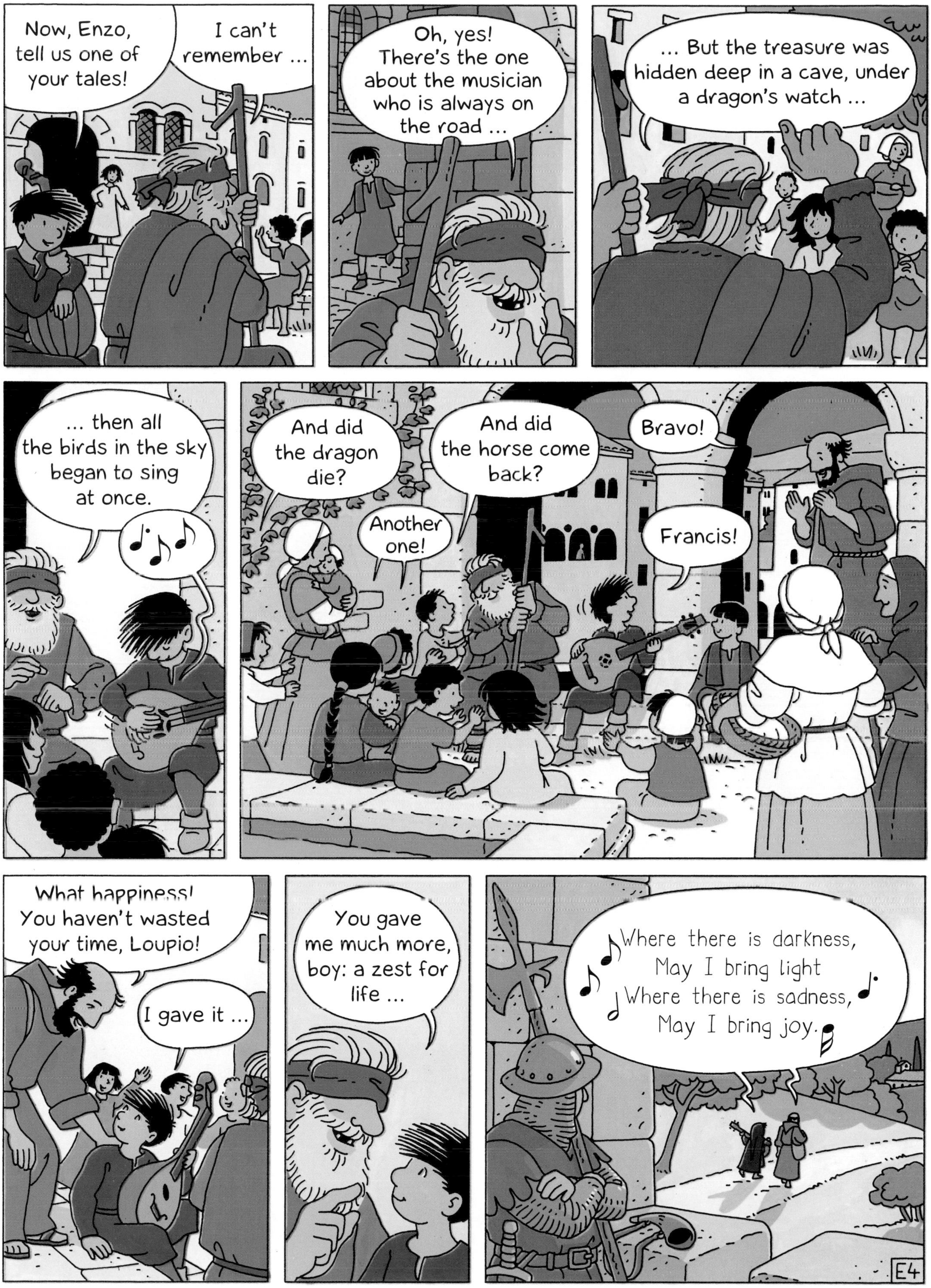
Now, Enzo, tell us one of your tales!
I can't remember ...
Oh, yes! There's the one about the musician who is always on the road ...
... But the treasure was hidden deep in a cave, under a dragon's watch ...
... then all the birds in the sky began to sing at once.
And did the dragon die?
Another one!
And did the horse come back?
Bravo!
Francis!
What happiness! You haven't wasted your time, Loupio!
I gave it ...
You gave me much more, boy: a zest for life ...
Where there is darkness,
May I bring light
Where there is sadness,
May I bring joy.
E4

The Dungeon

♪ Listen to the song ♪ of a poor musician, neither parents nor home and always on the road. ♩

Brother Wolf, I'm going to try to earn a little money in this town. Wait for me nearby!

A musician! I love musicians!

Hello, I'm Hugo, son of the lord of the castle ...

Uh, I'm Loupio!

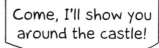

Come, I'll show you around the castle!

Here is my family's coat of arms ...

Here are my ancestors ...

And here is my father!

C 1

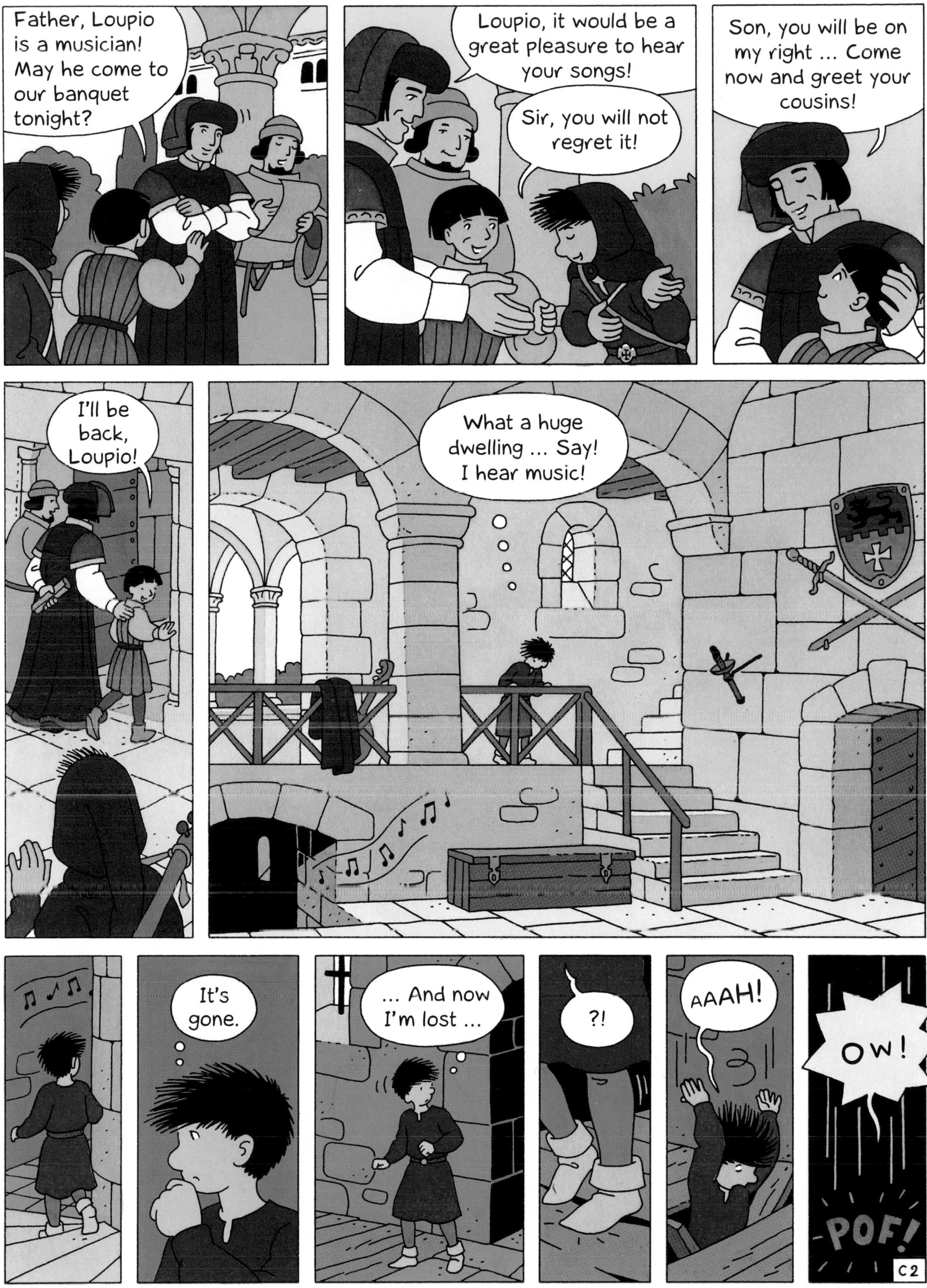

Father, Loupio is a musician! May he come to our banquet tonight?
Loupio, it would be a great pleasure to hear your songs!
Sir, you will not regret it!
Son, you will be on my right ... Come now and greet your cousins!
I'll be back, Loupio!
What a huge dwelling ... Say! I hear music!
It's gone.
... And now I'm lost ...
?!
AAAH!
OW!
POF!
C2

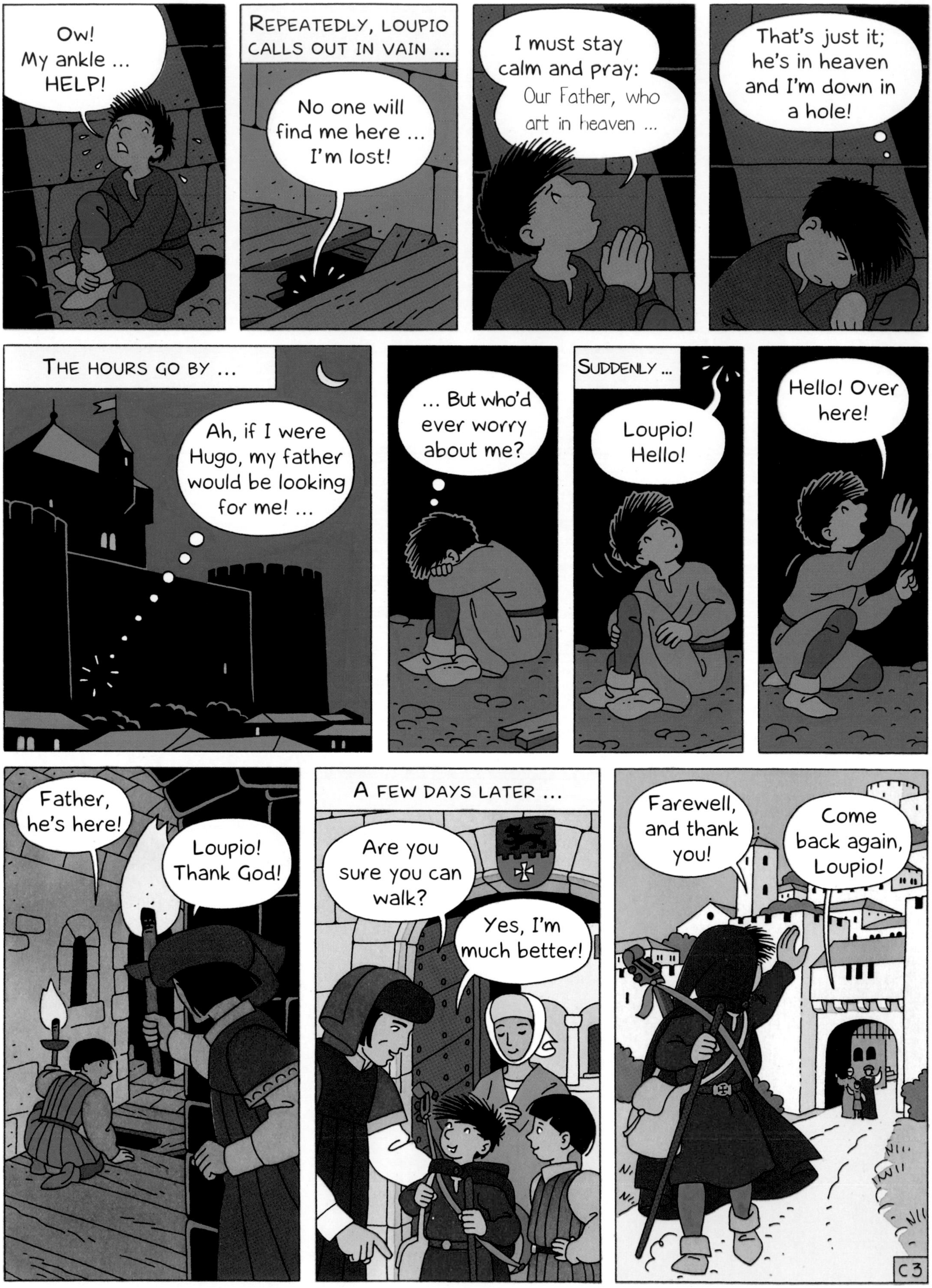
Ow!
My ankle ...
HELP!
Repeatedly, Loupio calls out in vain ...
No one will find me here ... I'm lost!
I must stay calm and pray:
Our Father, who art in heaven ...
That's just it; he's in heaven and I'm down in a hole!
The hours go by ...
Ah, if I were Hugo, my father would be looking for me! ...
... But who'd ever worry about me?
Suddenly ...
Loupio! Hello!
Hello! Over here!
Father, he's here!
Loupio! Thank God!
A few days later ...
Are you sure you can walk?
Yes, I'm much better!
Farewell, and thank you!
Come back again, Loupio!
C3

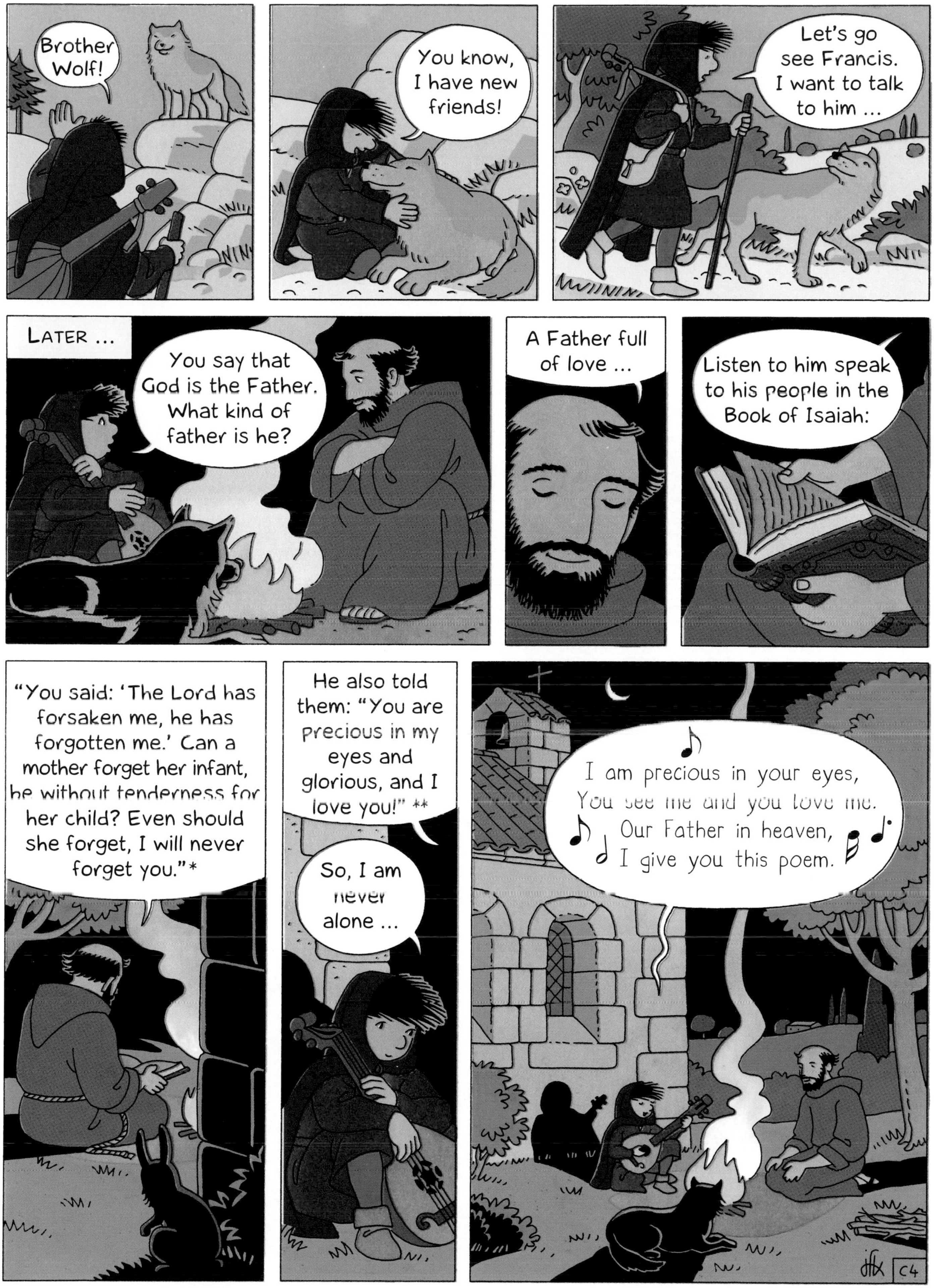
Brother Wolf!
You know, I have new friends!
Let's go see Francis. I want to talk to him ...
LATER ...
You say that God is the Father. What kind of father is he?
A Father full of love ...
Listen to him speak to his people in the Book of Isaiah:
"You said: 'The Lord has forsaken me, he has forgotten me.' Can a mother forget her infant, be without tenderness for her child? Even should she forget, I will never forget you."*
He also told them: "You are precious in my eyes and glorious, and I love you!" **
So, I am never alone ...
I am precious in your eyes,
You see me and you love me.
Our Father in heaven,
I give you this poem.

*Isaiah, chapter 49, verses 14 and 15

**Isaiah, chapter 43, verse 4

The Nativity Scene

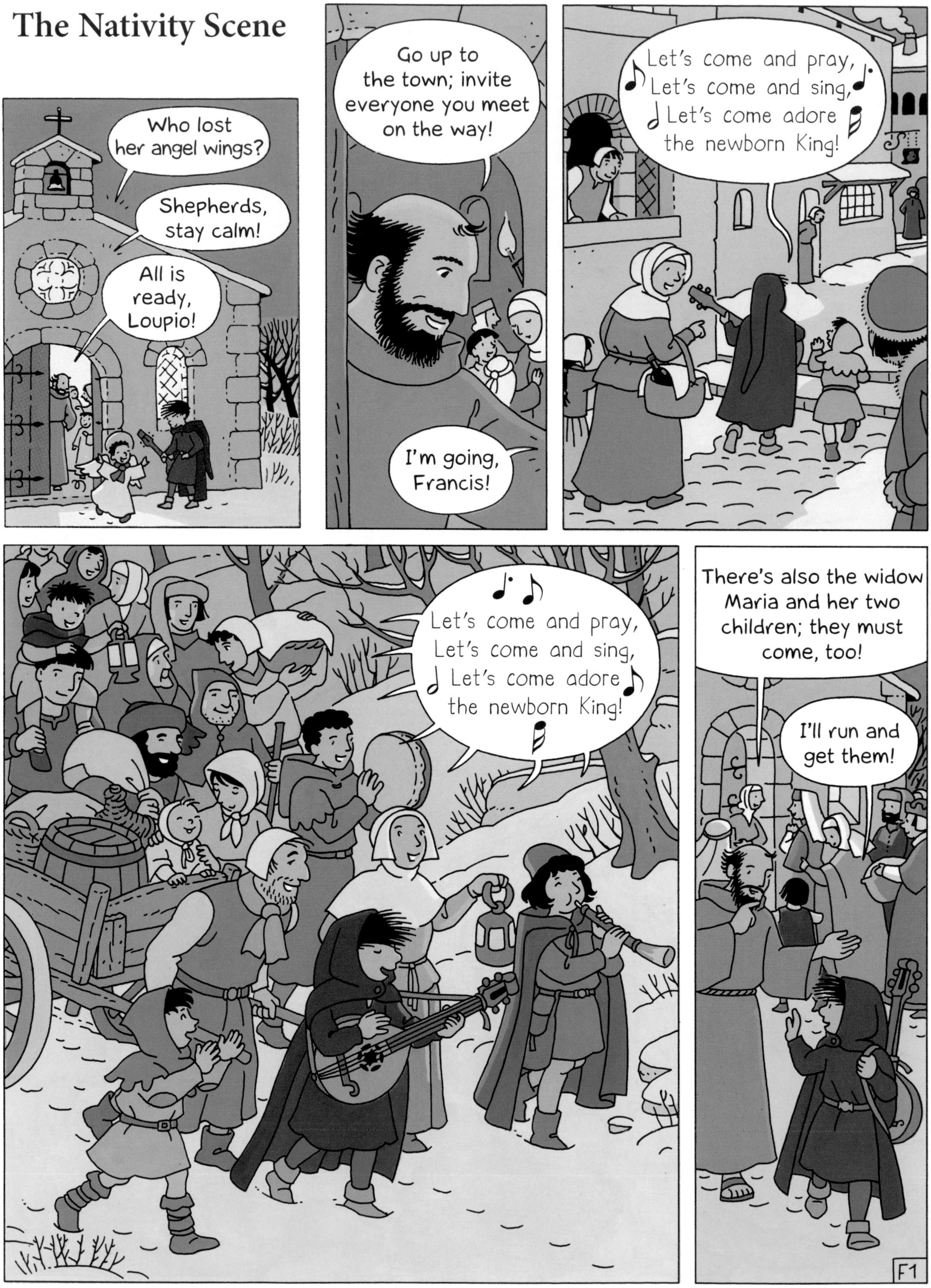
Who lost her angel wings?
Shepherds, stay calm!
All is ready, Loupio!
Go up to the town; invite everyone you meet on the way!
I'm going, Francis!
Let's come and pray, Let's come and sing, Let's come adore the newborn King!
Let's come and pray, Let's come and sing, Let's come adore the newborn King!
There's also the widow Maria and her two children; they must come, too!
I'll run and get them!
F1

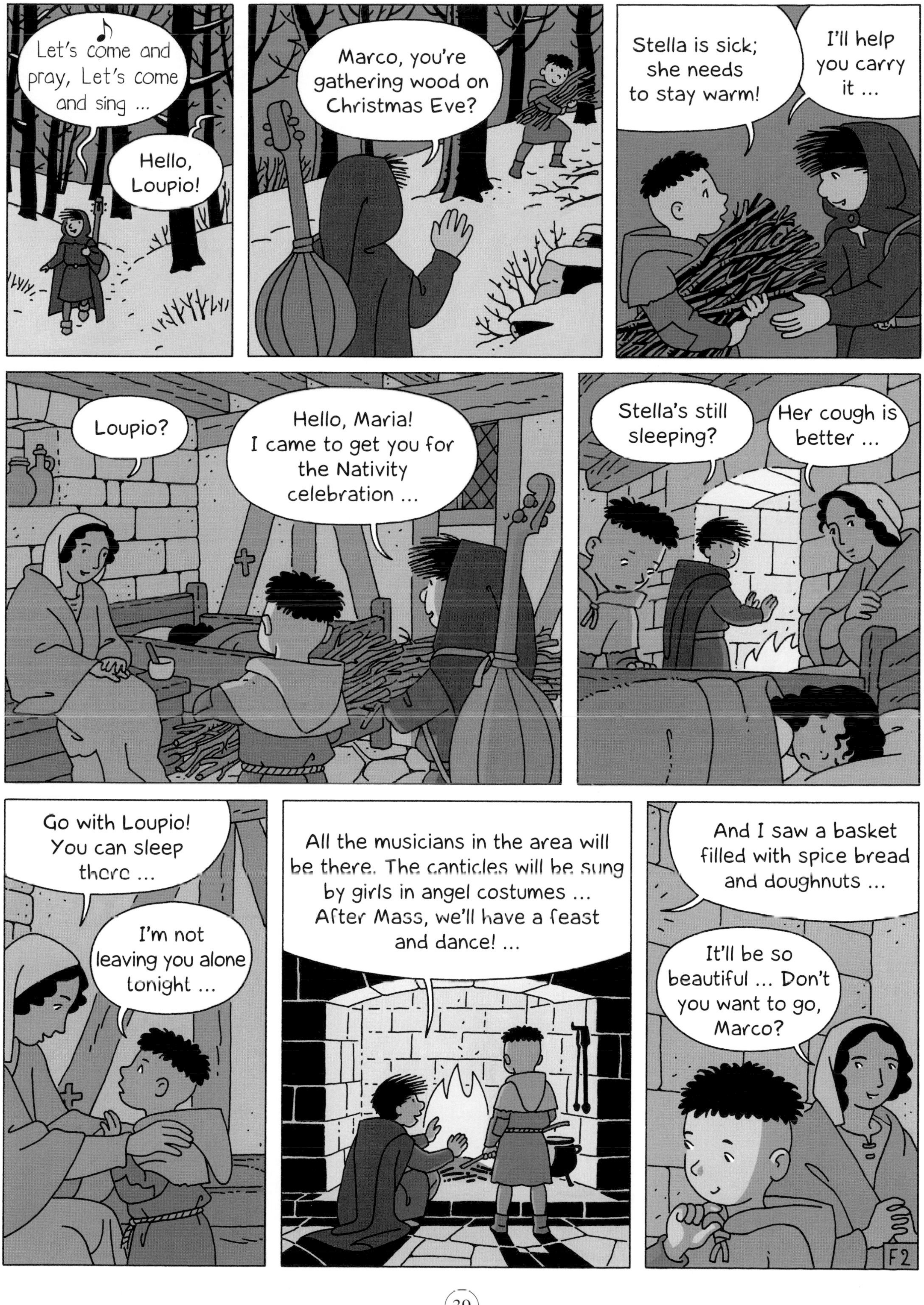
Let's come and pray, Let's come and sing ...
Hello, Loupio!
Marco, you're gathering wood on Christmas Eve?
Stella is sick; she needs to stay warm!
I'll help you carry it ...
Loupio?
Hello, Maria! I came to get you for the Nativity celebration ...
Stella's still sleeping?
Her cough is better ...
Go with Loupio! You can sleep there ...
I'm not leaving you alone tonight ...
All the musicians in the area will be there. The canticles will be sung by girls in angel costumes ... After Mass, we'll have a feast and dance! ...
And I saw a basket filled with spice bread and doughnuts ...
It'll be so beautiful ... Don't you want to go, Marco?
F2

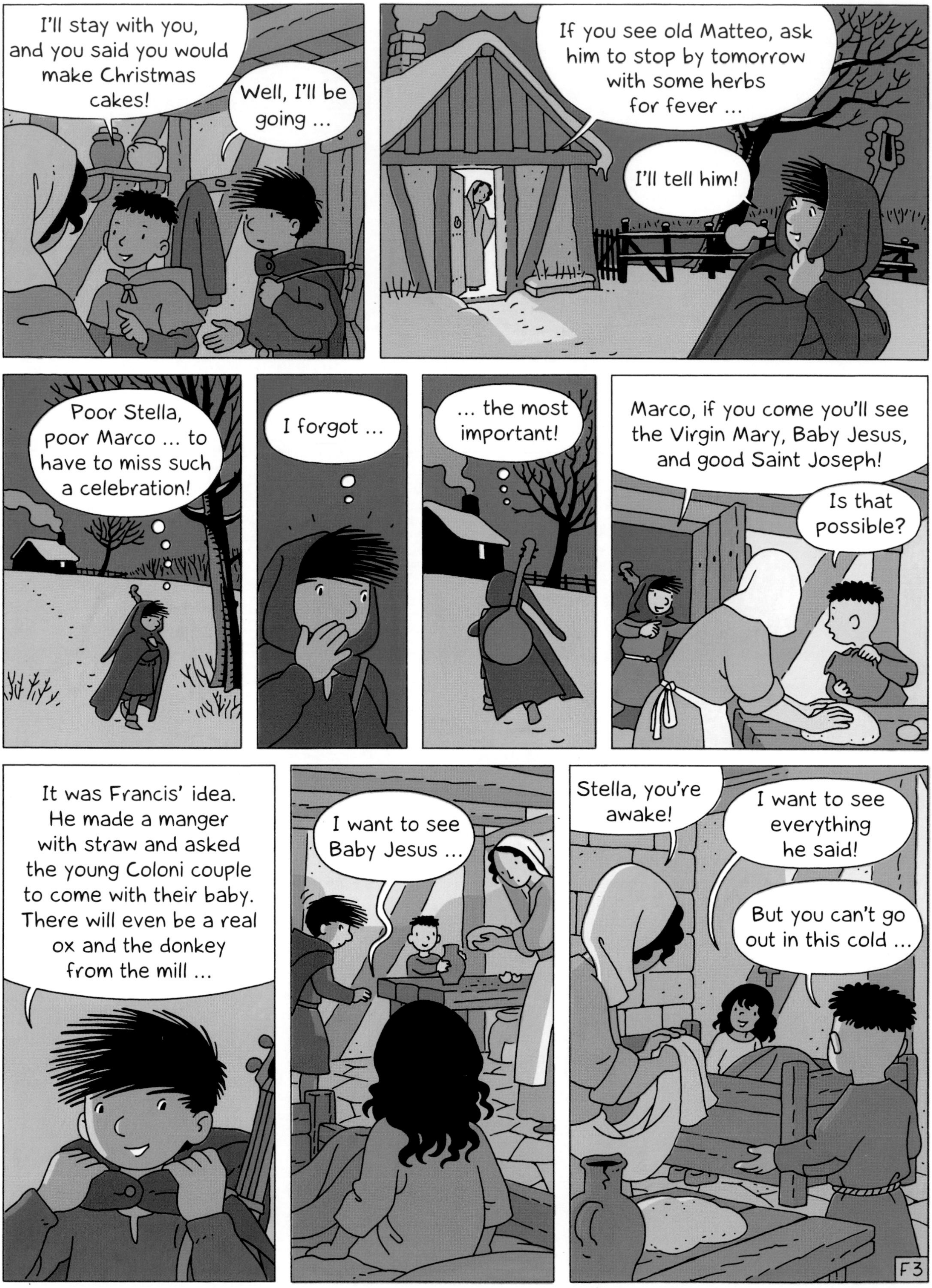
I'll stay with you, and you said you would make Christmas cakes!
Well, I'll be going ...
If you see old Matteo, ask him to stop by tomorrow with some herbs for fever ...
I'll tell him!
Poor Stella, poor Marco ... to have to miss such a celebration!
I forgot ...
... the most important!
Marco, if you come you'll see the Virgin Mary, Baby Jesus, and good Saint Joseph!
Is that possible?
It was Francis' idea. He made a manger with straw and asked the young Coloni couple to come with their baby. There will even be a real ox and the donkey from the mill ...
I want to see Baby Jesus ...
Stella, you're awake!
I want to see everything he said!
But you can't go out in this cold ...
F3

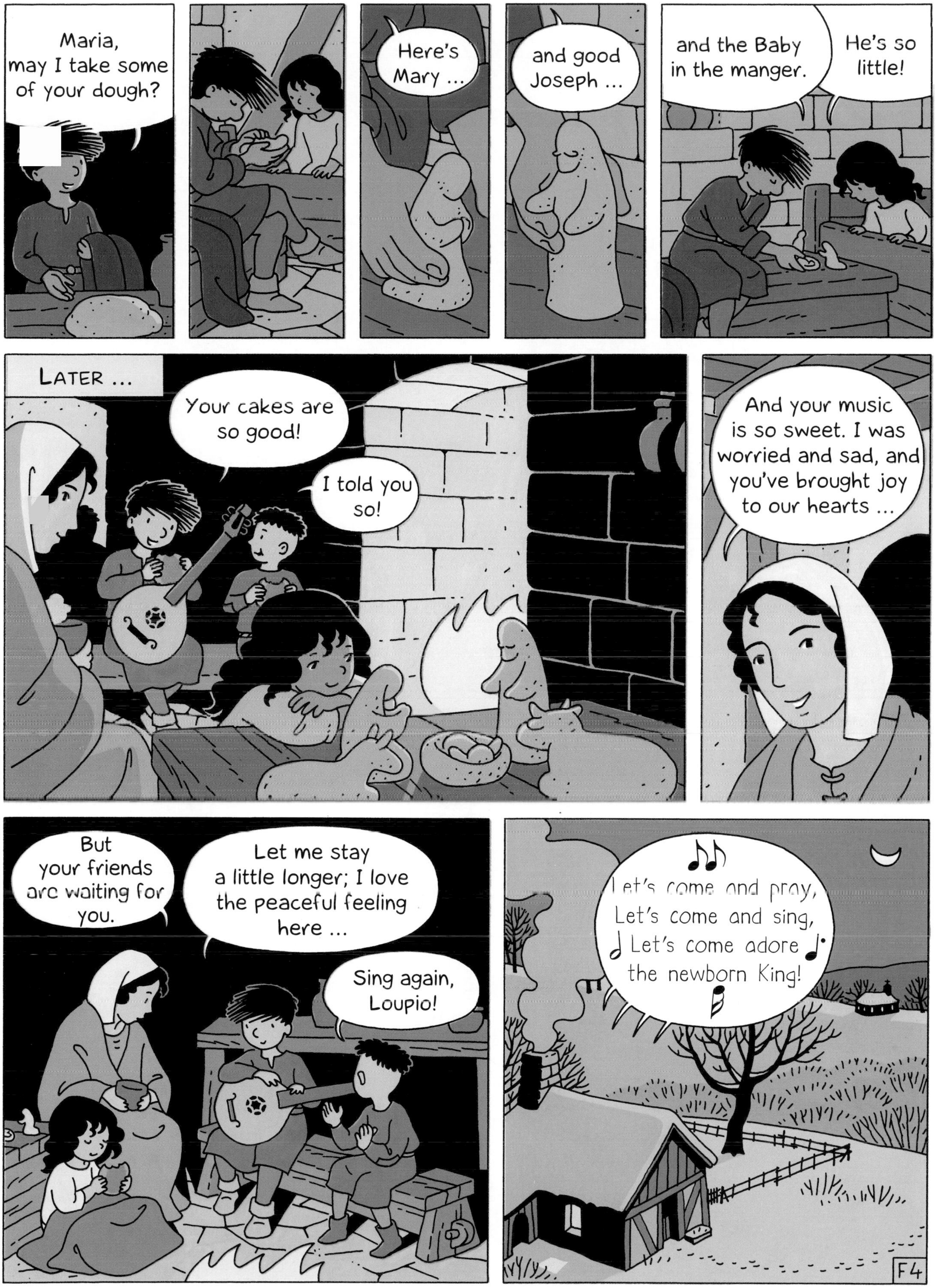
Maria, may I take some of your dough?
Here's Mary ...
and good Joseph ...
and the Baby in the manger.
He's so little!
LATER ...
Your cakes are so good!
I told you so!
And your music is so sweet. I was worried and sad, and you've brought joy to our hearts ...
But your friends are waiting for you.
Let me stay a little longer; I love the peaceful feeling here ...
Sing again, Loupio!
Let's come and pray,
Let's come and sing,
Let's come adore
the newborn King!
F4

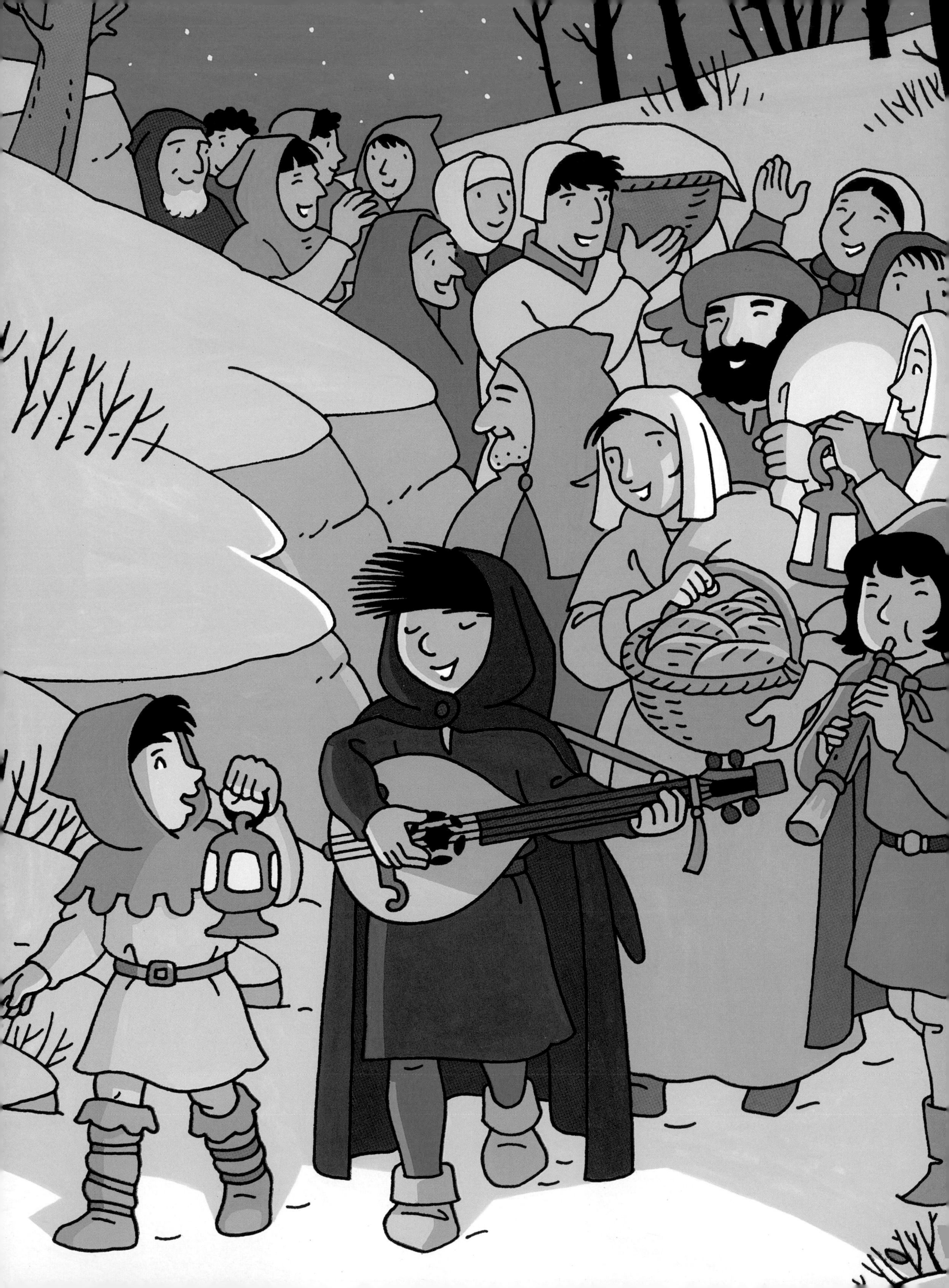

Loupio's Christmas

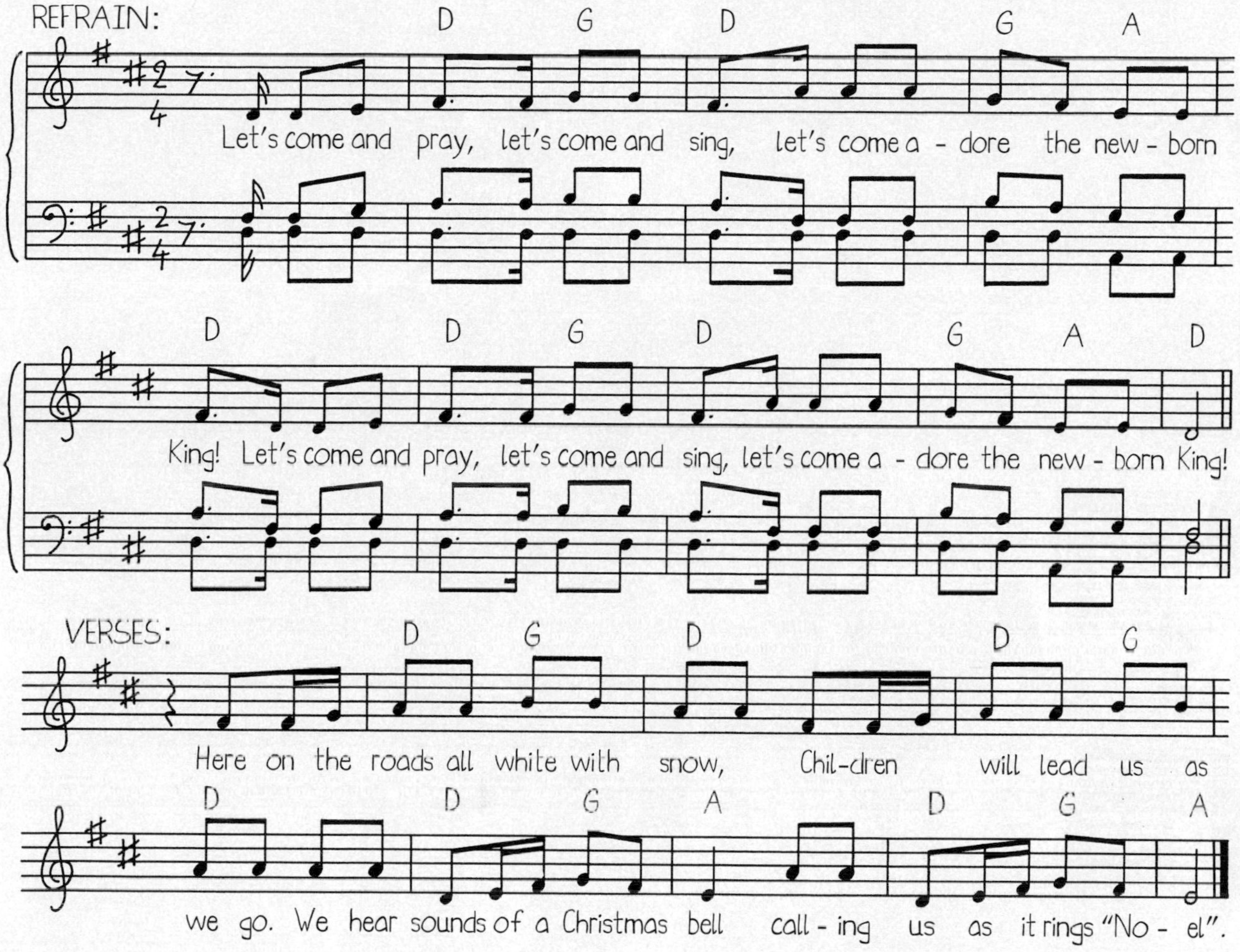
REFRAIN:
D G D G A
Let's come and pray, let's come and sing, let's come a - dore the new - born
D D G D G A D
King! Let's come and pray, let's come and sing, let's come a - dore the new - born King!
VERSES:
D G D D G
Here on the roads all white with snow, Chil-dren will lead us as
D D G A D G A
we go. We hear sounds of a Christmas bell call - ing us as it rings "No - el".

Here on the roads all white with snow,
Children will lead us as we go.
We hear sounds of a Christmas bell
Calling us as it rings "Noel".

We are the merchants here to sing.
Almonds and figs are gifts we bring.
Honor Jesus so small and great!
Join us now as we celebrate!

Sounds of the flute now fill the air,
Calling the sheep and goats all there.
See the shepherd with staff in hand
As he carries his youngest lamb.

Farmers with hay approach the shed
To find the manger now a bed!
He is God, but he sleeps right here
in the arms of his mother dear.

Here comes the baker with a treat:
Plenty of food for all to eat!
She brings rolls, loaves of bread, and cake.
Joyful evening, there's no mistake!

We are the guards and soldiers strong.
Without our swords, we sing this song.
He ends war and makes fighting cease.
This young boy is the Prince of Peace.

We are the beggars and the poor.
With empty hands we ask for more.
Without manners or voices skilled,
We rejoice as our hearts are filled.

As we announce this Good News proudly,
We entertainers don't sing loudly.
We sing softly with reverence deep;
Baby Jesus may be asleep!

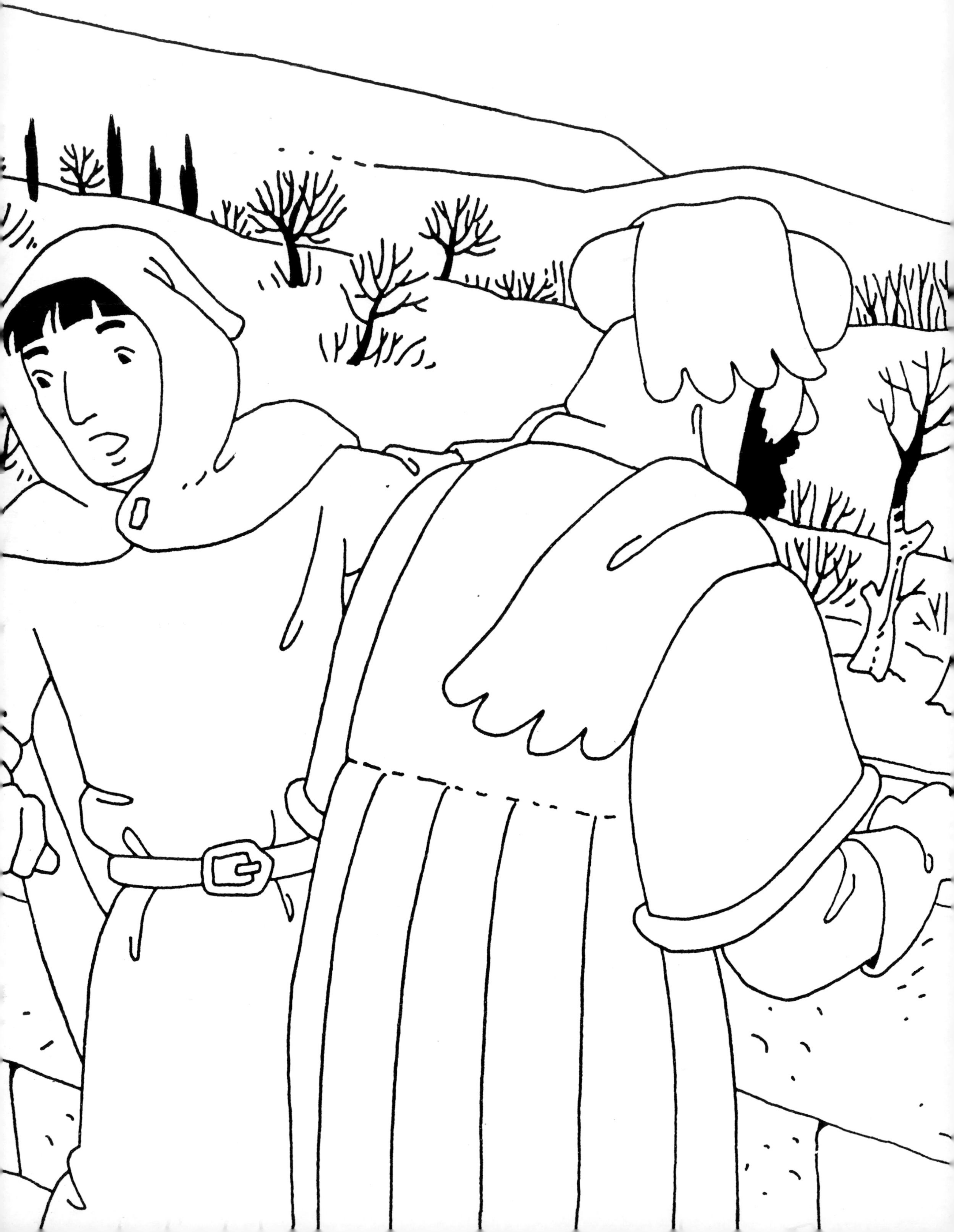